THE DEFIANT LIGHT

EVOCATIVE CREATIVE FICTION FROM THE EDGE OF LIFE

VICTOR D SANDIEGO

DYNAMIC CREED PUBLICATIONS

THE DEFIANT LIGHT

ISBN: 978-0-9905335-2-8

Meet The Standard Disclaimer

It's in the subtitle but to repeat: this is indeed a work of fiction. All of it. There might be some resemblance to actual persons who are presently in the world, or were in the world before, that is to say living or dead, but that would be only a coincidence. Same with places. References to actual places are used in a fictitious manner whether those actual places are actually beautiful, attractive, merely nice, or any other subjective description. And businesses, same idea, used in a fictitious manner. Please enjoy this work of the author's imagination.

Photos and art work by Victor D Sandiego

If I got rid of my demons, I'd lose my angels.

–Tennessee Williams

INTRODUCTION

Welcome. Although some of the stories in this collection are from an earlier period of my writing, the majority of them came forth in the last year or so, that is 2023 and the ending part of 2022. I'm grateful to have had the voices calling and the support with which to get them down on paper.

A great deal of my writing is concerned with the human condition and how we, as inhabitants of the earth, share many of the same celebrations, fears, desires, and setbacks. My wish in my writing is to offer a perspective that gets us thinking about what we do and what we're capable of doing. People have said that my work is parable in nature, and I suppose I can accept that.

On these pages, you'll get a look into various odd situations, some introspective, some externally focused, some in madness, others in peace, and a few whimsical ones as well. Each one has something to say, but that part isn't up to me. That's up to you the reader to enjoy and interpret in your own way. People have expressed to me the meaning they've gathered from my stories, and I'm always pleased to hear their interpretations because it gives me a new perspective with which to see the world, too.

Please enjoy, and all the best.

Victor David Sandiego

CONTENTS

THE DEFIANT LIGHT

VICTOR D SANDIEGO

TERMINAL LOS ANGELES

Night. He pushed the old car hard for the shipyards. Missed an onramp out of San Fernando, dropped onto the streets of Van Nuys. Rushed when he could down the carchoked boulevard. At stops his redlight brakefoot edgy, eager to free the engine from its idle.

Crime scene ahead. Ambulance, stretchers, sheets. He took a hard left on Magnolia, ran deeper into the body of the night. Cop said driving too fast but we'll let it go this time. A shared forearm tattoo. Brother both victims of the same wargod pressgang that flew home so damn many coffins.

Radio played a soft song but no soft thought at night in the terminal city. Slap knob radio silence. He pushed the old car hard for the shipyards.

His fear suffocation. It always came too soon. Six months, maybe ten and whatever ground he walked upon choked him in dust. Too many cries in his head. Too many calls to die in a desert of strip malls. Routine robbed him of essence.

He took the bypass to Burbank. A scrap of girl stood by the freeway sign. An extended and altogether holy thumb. Brakelights flashed and she entered. He pushed the old car hard for the shipyards.

What's your name? he asked but she answered that names are inventions. Pragmatic creations to seduce our isolation into surrender. He said okay I accept that. We choose our beliefs in shadows where the streetlights die.

They sat quiet and tires spun a story of distance between boredoms. A tale of traps.

Outside Glendale she pulled a cigarette from a bag, lit it hard and spoke of a Nebraska farm. They wanted her in the farmgirl role but she ran fast for the coast. This city of light and angels she said, full of small places to hide in the darkness.

Yes, he said and told her of his dream to have a heart that didn't beat the door down every few months demanding answers.

That's how we roll, she said and he knew she was right. The first time he killed a man he thought he would never stop dying. Stomach pains. God's deafness. But crusts grew over him with years like barnacles and he found ships of other restless men to bear him to another shore.

Not hunting redemption, he said. Just a sense of place. The girl nodded with wisdom more expansive than her years. She too beheld her choices and longed. A family is not always blood.

On their right Elysian Park at night its secrets shrouded. Where are you going, she asked and he said I'm too tired from running to care. But Long Beach has ships and piers and one of them will have me. A deckhand or a long night swim.

Can we get a Coke? she asked and he said why not and they pulled off on another stale Main St. with its own sort of killing fields. A store illumed and stocked to the top like heaven, the clerk a dark youngbeard still in the thrall of being. Back on the road, tincan condensation on his fingers, he pushed the old car hard for the shipyards.

The girl became a light he could not witness blinded by his faulty wired ambition and she told him of a time she went to church in Nebraska with a father who put his hand under her blouse. To reach into the house of the lord.

That is a man I would kill, said the man. The old car growled.

No need. He passed out in a wheat field of combines.

My daughter ran from my death wish, he said.

Where is she now?

Upstate. Inland. Far from ships.

Three miles of silence in the city of unincorporated dreams. Red yellow white car lights. A ten lane conduit between existence and extinction. Five million axles each day this path. Each a savage homecoming fraught with survival. Week to week. Small sidelined houses and dead roses. Concrete blocks. Sins of the road.

And you? asked the man. Me what? Where going?

San Pedro, said the girl. A night job. She lit another smoke.

Inside her voice dwelled sad desperation. Born of highways and cheap motels. Truckers and backcab beds. To do what you must to cross the tangled wilds of America. To pace through the city of angels in search of blessing. A beaten remedy. Chunks of doubt.

The man sought a ship. Salvation wasn't his to possess. His choices had ruled that out long ago but he still carried light into dim alleys of his life to see what vagrants slept in cardboard shelters of his past. Awake in the middle of the night to reach for a weapon. To grasp a gunblack savior when midnight trashtrucks hammered the dumpsters.

What kind of job, he asked the girl but she wouldn't say. Only that it kept her alive in the terminal city. A job condemned, a vacancy filled. A dark angelthing best left unworded in the night as he pushed the old car hard for the shipyards.

They passed Pico Gardens, Boyle Heights. You and I aren't freight trains, he said. Moving goods. And the girl blew smoke through the cracked vent window into a faithful slipstream. We're not, she said. But I don't know what else to do.

Come with me, he said. Why? I lied, said the man. What about? My daughter. What about her? And the girl tossed the last of her cigarette into the road where it short sparked and quick drafted onto the shoulder with other discards in the terminal city.

She tried to soothe my disease, said the man. Baptize it. But I pushed her away.

Go back to her. Explain your love.

Too late. She took a bad injection.

And now you run.

Yes, he said and swerved a lane to catch the ramp to the 710. Now I run. And he pushed the old car hard past rusted trains and concrete rivers. He pushed a final straight shot to the shipyards.

Then take me with you, the girl said and the man said yes. A ship brings relief. Release. It buries ended love and old regret at sea.

The girl nodded knowing and the night moved on down the freeway and spread into a hundred cargoed vessels on their way to a foreign coast. Bound for a port of belief that life must one day hold intent. Out past Signal Hill in the consuming rush to leave the terminal city to its death the man and girl felt the harbor lights brush their eyes and heard the sound of diesels driving props. Submerged in a sea of distant prospects they battled to stay that final breath. Lung's betrayal or life's reward. They pushed the old car hard. As hard as they could. Hard as they might for the shipyards.

HOW CLOUDS BECAME HIS CRADLE

In the early predawn light of Indiana Route 161, as his late model car slammed into the side of a tractor trailer rig at 69 mph, shearing off the top of the car and leaving its decapitated chassis to screech beneath the truck and gradually slow and finally come to a stop on the side of the highway, William J. Cooper thought about the time his father had taken him to the circus and how he, with his childish sense of wonder fully intact, had marveled at the lion trainer.

How does he do it, Papa? he had asked. The lion trainer had his head inside the sharp guarded cave of the lion's mouth.

He accepts the risk, his father replied.

Some words float away, but as happens at times, his father's words entered the creviced folds of William's impressionable mind and took refuge there. They incubated and slowly extended tendrils until they were firmly latched and he understood with both his heart and humanity what his father had meant.

On his eighteenth birthday, deep in the California Santa Cruz mountains, William J. Cooper climbed an enormous Redwood tree until he could encircle its trunk with his thumb and forefinger. His feet rested on birdbone thin branches and his body swayed from side to side in the secret upper chambers of the sky.

A snapped branch would surely shred his body into scrapmeat as gravity ordered limb after lower limb to claim its transit toll, but he accepted the risk.

The next day, William took a bus to Camp Pendleton and joined the Marines. They taught him how to run through mud, and without compassion point a rifle at another human being and squeeze the trigger. A danger lurked for him, as it did for the entire company, that the same squeeze would wring the lifeblood from their empathy, but he accepted the risk.

Three years later, his temperament steeled and deepened, William J. Cooper stepped off a military transport plane in North Carolina and returned to civilian life. Out there, in the world of unregimented opportunity, he would be on his own. He accepted the risk.

William made his way on foot north into the Appalachian Mountains where days ran like rivers through him and bears occasionally sniffed his shirt. He thought himself an undisruptive intruder into their habitat, and even though he couldn't know if the wildlife sensed his peaceful intention, he accepted the risk.

Back in Indiana, as his car screeched beneath the tractor trailer, tearing the final roof from his world, William J. Cooper had an instant – due to the immense capacity of the human spirit in catastrophic throes to stretch a second into a lifetime – in which to appreciate the summer day in Cheyenne, Wyoming when an old man had approached him and asked William for help.

William had spent the last few years drifting from one vague discontent to another and didn't have much to offer, but he paused, set his backpack on the sidewalk, and let the workers hurry past to their paycheck prisons.

What do you need? William asked and the old man replied that he needed to move a couch and several heavy boxes and that his strength had betrayed his bones and that he didn't have any money but that he could offer William a place to stay for the night and a simple hot meal.

Have you no friends? asked William and the old man said no. Have you?

For an instant the old man's eyes flickered sparking Indiana truck steel, then guttered. William agreed to help. They climbed three flights of stairs where William learned, after moving the couch and the boxes, that the old man called himself Benjamin and that for many years, long ago, he had worked in the circus with lions.

You accepted the risk, said William.

Benjamin set a plate of beans in front of William, sat, opened a beer. I did, he said.

Outside Topeka, Kansas, a hardnotched tattooed man with a gun on the seat picked up hitchhiker William on I-70 and William rode a dicey encounter into Junction City with muffled thumps coming from the trunk, but the present moment hurled the severed margins of William's memory faster and faster beneath the Indiana truck trailer and Kansas disappeared.

With only faint sparkles of a split second left to recall how he zigzagged his life across America in search of possibility and understanding, William J. Cooper summoned the face of the woman who touched his afternoon heart when they drank coffee on a terrace of bountiful flowers.

They spread sweet butter on toast and took their vows to a home filled with love in Indiana where they settled down, adopted a dog, created a daughter, bought a late model car, and where William's neck strings, like those of an over tuned violin, snapped one by one on Route 161 at 69 mph in the rushing dawn.

And as the light began to imperceptibly shift from reddish to a hazy cerulean that heralds for many their first or last earthly day, and the truck driver jump startled at the screams that a metal cage of car makes when it peels open like onionskin to expose the human layers within, the consciousness of William J. Cooper began its closing reflective journey into the slipstream.

A boy enthralled at the circus, an adolescent in a treepierced sky, a man who battled for his own peace within. Consumed in the perfect ecstasy of sadness, all their shared wisdom melded into a single fleshy head of blood and mist that rose higher and higher into the pale Indiana heavens. Clouds became his cradle and the great affairs of love, opportunity and danger that life serves us all on a platter of days, his first and final companions.

NONE OF THIS MAKES SENSE

The man came home. Like many do. Tired of his job. His life. The rent due and a bank account barely. A movie on TV and he watched it without watching. Some old black and white thing about a man who came home to a satchel of money in his bedroom because he had robbed a thief.

It didn't make sense. The man came home like so many come home. From the movies with popcorn in their teeth or from work with dread in their heart. Movies. Life. They don't make sense. Maybe the man got off at the wrong stop when he left work. Or the movie. Life just the flip side of death.

He didn't even know what he meant. Movie or job or man on TV who stole money from a thief. A series of events, like most life. Go here. Go over there. Find a job, come home to the microwave, make some popcorn. Watch something on TV.

Life plus death equals existence.

It doesn't make sense.

And why should it. The man who came home tired of his job learned a long time ago that a job gave him just enough money to survive, have shelter and food in between shifts at a job. There's a word for that.

We narrators know all the words but sometimes must keep quiet in case the man who came home tired of his job gets the wrong idea and considers revenge. Futile, but he might consider it. Revenge on the system, his job, his life. He might do a rampage when he sees the loop that never breaks out of its cycle. Spins only on the axle of his apartment, work, grocery store, TV, bed, work, grocery store.

Ever cycling into the core where death lives.

That doesn't make sense, said the man.

Correct. It doesn't make sense. But death is a living thing too. It crawls in through the window at night. Open or closed doesn't matter to death. Climbs in our ear and whispers funny little stories of a man stuck on a treadmill.

One time the man came home from work tired of his job as usual and ate a bunch of pills. But they didn't take. Didn't invite death in for the last supper. Oh Jesus. In the morning he had a headache and had to run for the bus. At work a woman said you look terrible and he said I feel terrible and she said I've got to get back to my cubicle.

An interrupted routine gave the man hope and he left work to look for a thief to rob. But he didn't know any thieves. He only knew his coworkers and the guy at the grocery store. His family cuddled death under weathered tombstones and he sat on the edge of the world alone. He paid his rent, ate bread from the grocery store. And microwave popcorn. And watched TV without watching. To pass the time until the clock said bed and he went there to grasp the pillow and whisper oh god there must be more than this.

We narrators don't get union rates. But the man with the tiresome job who watches another man rob a thief on TV is our solemn responsibility. We must care for him. He is only alive because we said so. Continue to say so. Change the words and kill the man. How's that for power and sacred trust.

The man got up in the morning and said this is the day that I change the story. He walked down to the sidewalk and turned left instead of right. He walked three blocks and entered a liquor store. Give me your money, he said to the guy behind the counter. If I can't find a thief, I'll become one. And the guy behind the counter said we don't have any money because it's still early and most people don't start drinking until noon. And the man said okay. I'll come back later.

It doesn't make sense. Never did. We narrators try our best to tell everybody to enjoy life and don't worry about whether you understand it or not, but most people, like the man who went to the liquor store instead of work, don't listen. They clamp their hands tight on their head and whisper oh god there must be more than this.

After the liquor store, the man walked down to another bus stop for another bus to another part of the city where he didn't work. When he got there he jumped off and asked the people on the sidewalk where he was and they said lost.

But I'm looking for death, he said.

That's a strange wish, said a dreadlocked girl.

Not really, said the man. I must confront it.

Two blocks over, said someone and the man walked two blocks over. A sign read Psychiatrist. Close enough. He entered and sat in a chair with his arms floppy folded like dirty laundry and told the psychiatrist he had a dream.

What dream? she asked.

A gigantic plate of glass at least a foot thick falls from a construction site, he said. It bounces once or twice and then flattens me beneath it where I can see translucent sky.

That sounds scary.

But then a giant hand lifts the glass away and I'm transported to a room with god drinking a cup of tea.

That doesn't make sense, said the doctor psychiatrist.

But what does it mean?

It means we all die one day.

The man stood up. I'm not paying for that, he said. And walked out.

In the street they were installing an enormous window in a ten story building with a giant crane. If that falls on me I'll die, said the man and a construction guy said that's right, better get out of here. But the man said I think I'll wait and see how it goes. Maybe this would be the final window that death crawls through.

That doesn't make sense, said the construction guy.

No it doesn't, said the man. But maybe death, like truth, would finally set him free. Let him open a vast window and jump into the arms of god just in time for tea.

It didn't need to make sense. It only needed to break the loop of life and death into a thousand rainbowed chunks of glass that he could then scatter into an endless sky. Life didn't have to have meaning. It only needed to be a little more cherished than death.

The Passages of War and Sickness

His beliefs are living beings, Holden says, talking about himself again. At first they fall as impoverished angels into his eyes as dawn paints the window reddish. Then they lather his daylight with hard thoughts of who should receive a suggestion of death and who a short sentence of life. They tumble into the crevices of his doubts, clamoring with their sharp edges of how he must rise and admire his administration of justice.

What's that? I say. You're not a great god, not even a mayor or a teacher. Only a failed novelist.

True, he says. But we all have more inside.

Give me more coffee, I say to the waiter. He bows and retreats to the kitchen.

It wasn't always like this. Before the world rolled clouds across the sky faster and made clocks our masters, we rode from one end of our neighborhood to another on bicycles, playing the pedals like drums. We pounded rhythms with a ferocity that thrust phantoms from our dreams and gave them flesh.

Holden clears his throat. Do you remember how we loved Antonio?

Of course, but where is he now?

He went to the revolution.

Yes. He went to march the hills in search of institutions to tumble. Yet I always wondered how he kept track of whose side he was on.

I tap the rim of my cup with a single finger. The waiter pours, bows only the required depth his duty demands, pads across the tile floor to check the street. Morning is still alive and people walk past maybe looking for work or a reason to go home and give up on the day.

And Martha the ghost? How she charged through the ghetto!

I remember, I say. It would be impossible, even irreligious, to forget.

The last time we spoke we sat on the curb under our street's only fruit tree. Oranges drooped from their branches, some of pale health, but many hearty and seemingly eager to burst into our waiting mouths with the sweet innocence of harvest. We talked of abundance and want, of war and other sickness. We promised to never give up.

Martha had gone to volunteer at the hospital.

Why do you want to be a nurse? a man asked. He was a middle-aged man with a mustache who was director of this or that.

It's our duty, Martha said. All of us must win this war.

Do you stand by our faith? The one that speaks in punishments and rewards. It gives and it takes away. Have you been to Calvary?

I don't know about those things, Martha said. My father was a doctor, though.

It's true. When we were little, Martha's father would knock on the door and then duck his head to come inside. He had thermometers and small vials of pills.

They didn't take her. Of surgeries and smocks they were sure. But they were afraid of contamination, afraid to infect their patients with ideas outside the borders of their faith. Better a failed body than a divergent soul.

But why didn't you pretend? I asked. I thought of an orange but we were seated and the branches were out of reach.

It's too hard.

I already knew that. I had tried to enlist in the guard but they wouldn't have me. I was the right age, young enough to run quickly yet insufficient of years to understand that wars aren't for soldiers or ideals. They're for library men in robes with their tea cups, and men in suits who hire staff to count their money. But I didn't know that then. I thought we should fight and maybe die to keep our constitution unharmed.

That's the spirit, the man of the guard had said. Before you get to thirty and start a family or a business, get out there and help repel foreign invaders.

Foreign invaders? I asked. We lived in a time of strength. None would dare.

It's simple to do what you're commanded, he said. That's the important part. Don't ask questions. Jump with much enthusiasm at the opportunity to help the nation in its time of need. When we are strong, we must protect our peace abroad. Do you understand?

Peace? I asked. I thought we were at war.

We're always at war. You just don't know it. There's hoards out there in the cold world who want to take what is yours.

My what?

They decided I wasn't fit. I went back outside and for a moment marveled at the rows of soldiers on the field, each aligned to the next, one indistinguishable from the other, like old women at their sewing machines in a clothing factory.

Yes, it's too hard, I said. Martha nodded.

When we stood up, Martha walked one way, I another. I would have looked back and waved if I had known what infirmity lay cancerous in her bones at that moment, ready to begin its treacherous journey into the heart of her good health. I would have given her a hug if I had known, a long wrap of love for our lives up until that moment, that we would each find a peace in the world and a place. That we would treat each day like a fresh fruit.

But I didn't, I say to Holden. My coffee is cool.

Oh? Do you regret her disappearance?

A little.

My beliefs are real, he says. Made of emeralds, just like yours.

I would build with mine if I could, I say. I would construct a jeweled palace where sickness could confine itself in splendor outside our bodies, the bodies of our families. And friends. Let flesh be free flesh, not burdened with the weight of famine or rotted with the dryness of thirst.

I finish my coffee. More, I say to the waiter. He bows and retreats to the kitchen.

That's not how it works, says Holden. We can't wall it off.

He's right of course. We can't. It's not possible to contain the drought that assaults us.

A spiritual drought, I say.

Holden puts two fingers on his temple. We can call it that, he says.

A sensation starts in my legs and moves up through my torso. They say that the soul dries before the spirit, that the soul moves through the body in search of nourishment and splendor. It's a warning sign, a wakeup that there's still time.

Yes, let's call it that, I say. It gives us something to hold onto.

Holden lowers his fingers, points them at my cup. I see streaks of marble in his eyes.

Outside, feet lightly pass. The impoverished angels of our lives hover. The waiter quietly pours.

THE SILENT SONS OF PROPAGANDA

When the people of Allentown stepped from the corners of their uncertain fear, the president promised in a voice that weaved a silken tapestry that he would bring an end to their world of distress, that he would free their world of its inscrutable pestilence. He only needed their help.

One young man stood quiet and still. His town, with its beautiful brickwork and iron railings, had become a part of him over the years, every curve and corner. Each tree and street had multiplied him.

Still, he knew what he must do. He stood with his throat full of birds on the edge of departure, a leaving to fulfill his duty. Despite the expectant swelling of his tongue, he bore no words but: goodbye.

Goodbye. The smooth sounds of assurance had persuaded him. Young men such as himself must carry a conflict to a faraway desert before those who stood outside his faith brought a battle to their own shores.

He had learned at an early age to accept the offered truth. It started with a father who brought the razor strap down where his spine shimmered bone and progressed through a series of ministers and teachers who at first begged, and later ordered him, to forsake his childish ideas of autonomy.

We are not our own masters, they said. We serve wiser guides.

The train carried him to the coast where a thousand other young men stood in loose lines waiting to board ships. All carried the same face, a face that a thousand clerics with a thousand rubrics had engraved with the hot threat of damnation. On each face an anxiety sat hunched and clearly visible in the dark lines that ran from the corners of their eyes into the folds of their mouths.

The young man turned. My name is..., he started to say to the boy who stood behind him, but an elder with stripes on his sleeves and a cross around his neck cut off his speech with a sharp rod on the wrist that cracked the morning into two divisions of silence and astonishment. The elder told him that names grew attachments and attachments beget questions and questions looked for answers where none were needed, or desired. The young man's mouth fell into muteness and he exhaled a single long breath of assent.

An old man climbed a platform and raised his arms. When each eye of each young face turned toward him, he lowered them. Across this sea, he said, kneel hoards of men who fell from grace and, if given a chance, would rip yours from your breast with long knives. To save ourselves and all the decency we represent, you must go to them.

For weeks the ships slow glided over gray seas. Meals below decks passed in silence as elders watched, and with their sharp rods struck each nascent word or question that formed a bubble on a lip. Aborted, sounds fell to the metal floors unspoken.

When they arrived, all the young men of a thousand fathers from a thousand towns stepped forward into the desert sun where their duty thickpressed them and imprinted its demands on their skin that pulsed raw and red as if from a beating.

The young man of Allentown who had left his home to join the crusade, looked around. Sand and sun marched, as they would march, over rows of dunes. Over there, he thought, somewhere far off still, sat foreign boys with foreign tongues who split their version of the sky with the same question:

Who am I? he asked.

But the question rose as Icarus toward the furnace of the sun and melted. Even if he had an answer, he had no way of knowing if he was right or wrong. The distinctions themselves lay convicted of treason in the unlit lower dungeons of his heart.

A horn blew. And another. Diesel engines rumbled to life. On the horizon fires burned. Every young man turned every young head with every young face to the east where their destiny sat surrounded by tombstones. The day of their days stood upon them.

Goodbye Rudy For Ships

Feels like San Pedro or Long Beach when I wake up: my tongue ripped thick with sea salt and diesel stink, eyes filled with yellow streetlight burlap sky. Rats gnawing ropes over by Terminal Way

in my head.

Two guys hurry past my bench with underbreath mumbles about bums.

What do they know? Ocean breeze is still free.

From St. Mary's, ambulances come and go. And they're not talking of Michelangelo no more with bar fights and numb junkies to heal.

Taxi drivers slap their meters down. Sailors laugh and burp beer.

But my big brother Rudy not coming back to unbend the skewed angle of my pain. He stuck his head into a goddamn military

lynching noose. Signed up to be a homeland hero.

On 10th St. I'm dripping sweat in my shoes. I spent my last paper bill for some paper bag wine to escort my toes packed in thin leather soles over sidewalk cracks

as quick knives of the night carve my heart up.

A discarded man knows how to stagger through parks and weave around pedestrians who got *their* loved ones back when the war finally busted.

They didn't pull last week's bread crumbs from their pockets and plant them on footpaths as benchmarks for a convoy of coffins to follow home. It's but a cruel joke because Rudy not coming back to caress my distress. He blew his big brother love into tree limbs above the tripwires.

At the docks, tall chain link and gray Navy ship hulls. And gulls crapsquawk white streaks on the foredecks when I hurl my empty bottle anger at those cold brass generals with fancy ribbons.

It's no good, though. They're bunkered down in far pentagons for sure and besides, my arc over razor wire is weak. Like pleading with giants from toadstools.

And right there, as a symbol of my soul, on the pavement, in sodium light between fence and dock, my wine bottle shatters.

I would fragment, too. Those last blood red drops drip from sad shards of myself. They slow crawl to the water like a stunted storm squall

and invite me to take communion with an emerald sea.

ALL OUR FALSE FACES

Night. Always night. We applied our masks, raised the curtain, crossed a stage and recited our lines. Instructed words, foretold. Within a dream within a conviction that a thespian forgery of life must upstage the ashen reality we performed outside the confines of the theater.

A play with three acts. Performed to perfection. In silence we thanked the audience as they in cacophony applauded our bows. Forever driven to the accolades of a faithless public. Tragedy. Comedy. Death and becoming. For two hours, we birthed distraction from our human isolation, allowed them and us to briefly both escape.

The curtain dropped. House lights came up. We removed our outer false faces and called out *good job* and *nice crowd tonight*. But as our recital in the theater was fiction, so was our ritual duty of blessings. We produced imaginary scenes in imaginary worlds with imaginary words. Only thing real was our avoidance of reality.

Tomorrow another show, another bid to please an exhausted world. I washed my inner false face, dressed in street clothes, left my castmates, exited the theater, walked an hourfull of city blocks to the home of my beloved.

She hung there still, a death shroud portrait upon the wall. Resplendent in the same Victorian dress she had worn on the last night we composed our love before her sickness grew bold. It wasn't a reunion. A rather goodbye. And I couldn't stay. Schedules to meet. A reckoning with truth beyond the stage door. A confession that my life outside the theater was also false.

I took her car. She had no say. Or didn't say because night darktumbled from God's hand and streetlights glowered. It doesn't need to make sense. A gun on the mantle must be discharged before the final stage light fades, but not even the playwright knows the bullet target until the script is laid to rest. Ashes of failures, one heap upon another. Blind soldiers marching to the gunner's nest.

I drove, soon was lost. The streets intersected in patterns I could not grasp. And the signs, though legible, bore no significance. My city, my beautiful sanctuary. I had crossed its stage over and over until each path bloomed a bloodline. But in this moment, my knowledge unborn. An outsider to my life.

Where must I go? I asked a man in a nightcloaked café. My car on the street, I had entered in hope. Please show me the way.

My hand pointed north but not because I knew it was true. A question. An attempt to prove my compass faithful, that I could still burrow my city and find its hidden holiness, that my arm could at least adopt a stance. Is that the way to my life? I asked.

The man in the café shook his head.

My perished role real, confirmed, my allied extras played their part. These hollow bones of thoughts followed me back to my car. But its tires spun in shallow quicksand, threw their vexation into the wheelwells. Though I believed in traction, it had no faith in me.

A woman stopped her car. I'll help you, she said, and for a moment I transported to an earlier arena of my life. I had been lost then too and an angel had thrown me a lifeline. An angel had guided me through an abyss and set free my mind.

Different this. An urban scene of a Platonic tragedy outside a café on the city stage. Not only myself but a hundred thousand souls lost in isolation. In poverty and desperation. My small suffering could not compare. An actor who declaimed words of another. Consummate words not my own. The player a mere shadow of the creator.

Get in, the woman said. She slid over. You drive.

With unfamiliar hands I drove us to the fringes of the city where industrial street-lights sprawl. Yellowish incandescence provided a milky promise of prosperity on the loading docks.

Where are we going? I asked.

Turn right at the bottom of hill.

To spin the wheel. To have no choice. To follow unmapped streets in search of my warrant. The woman told me left. Then told me right. We wove deeper into the silent industrial corpus, a Goliath without a David, my voice without a mouth.

Lost within the labyrinth of my uncertainty. This maze of streets. I drove on, bested by my barren choices. A crawl through an urban earth in search of God and my lung laced with suffocation.

The woman. My only guide, my final deliverance. Now, over there, she said, her finger extended. There we peel our disguised faces. There our final stage conducts us and strips us of deception.

Stop, she said. Get out. Now stand in the light. Here, in this spectacular light.

And light fell down upon me. More than my eyes could see.

Now, said the woman. Remove all your false faces. Turn from the audience of fools. It's time to reap the reward of the light, to praise this most singular opening night.

THE BEAUTIFUL LOPSIDED EYES OF TRIGGER GUARDS

Learned a long time ago that people want to hear what they want to hear, not what you really think, so when my father asked me how I was doing, living on the edge of nineteen years under the sun, cut off from the world, unsung and alone, I told him fine, mentioned nothing of the volcano that babbled inside me, furious and ready to erupt but somehow calm, methodical, because a volcano carries no malevolence for its victims, only an uncontrollable desire to breach its confines and redspread its hot seed over the land.

My father nodded and went back to his newspaper, an old fashioned guy, still paid for paper, and I rose from the porch where we were sitting and looked up at the sky that looked down with its dark clouds like it wanted to swallow kids like me and then spit them out because we don't belong here and we don't belong there either. We leave a bad taste wherever we go.

Down at Sam's I found beauty in handguns and rifles that pled with the lopsided eyes of their trigger guards for me to remove them from their pegs on the wall, to liberate them from the glass barriers that kept them from the public air. Their sleek metal lines caused my hunger to swell and I bought two grand ones, two exquisite examples of manufactured love.

Equipped, I knew the power of the unstoppable. An upheaval of oak trees filled my legs and my heart with hardness.

A volcano is fixed, bound to its birth home and therefore cannot choose its target, but I had the advantage of mobility. And the disguise of innocence. I could go where my lust could be best discharged from its prison. A bookstore, a schoolyard, a church, a shopping place. Any would do. I only needed to fill my isolation with gunpowder and spark the fuse. I would turn my facelessness to fame.

A mall. Before I entered, I paused in the parking lot to check my bag, to make sure my emancipators were prepared to tackle the tough questions a straitened outsider such as myself always has on the tip of their tongue such as who am I, and why does nobody like me? They were ready, my solemn validators, to make my quest for a purpose real.

Now for the hard part. To choose. A girl over there who wears the same mask as a girl who told me no? An old man on a bench with the air of someone who beats his children with harsh words and tells them constantly they'll never rise from the mud and shit they slid into by an accident of birth, even though none of this is their fault?

When the clock strikes the hour, it tells those with the courage to listen to stand up and terminate the tragedy that began on the birthbed nineteen years ago when they slapped an infant boy into consciousness and told him to get moving. Your womb loafing days are over. All the breast milk has dried into sheetstains. You're on your own.

That much is true. I'm on my own. Nobody told me I could and nobody told me I couldn't. From here, each step, each squeeze, each scream, each sound of a watermelon dropped on the floor as a body gives in to gravity, belongs to me.

At last. I am the taker. I am the owner of unspent lives.

Come to me, Mother. See what I have done. Kiss me on the forehead where the hot cross of your god once cattlestamped me.

And now. Now I belong to a scorching wind, one that blows me onto headlines for a week or two until another young man, and another, and another, all like me, all brothers of the same abandonment, of the same sickness, follow my path as I have followed those before me, that we may kill ourselves of what we have become, and join hands in the final circle of our sacred madness.

SOCIAL PROGRESS AT THE BUS STOP

Every morning, Indians. As I wait for the bus, a coffee in my hand, Indians. They come from the alley next to the pawn shop. Chief wears newspapers and duct tape. I'm unclear what we've done. Or if I'm guilty.

"Good morning Chief," I say. "What's the plan?" Same thing I say every morning.

"No plan," says Chief. His tribesmen nod. Everyone has mud on their shoes.

"Then what?"

"It's time you called me God," he says.

I laugh, spill a little coffee. The bus is almost here.

Chief touches my shoulder. "One more time and I'll kill you," he says.

"One more time what?"

"One more time you forget our history."

***

At the office, I ask Claire. "Claire, have you ever known a redskin?"

"We don't say that any more," she says.

"What do you mean?"

"We don't say what our eyes see."

But that's not what I wondered. I wondered if we have become our own fear, our own failure.

"Go back to work," says Claire.

Back at work, I ask an immigrant. His papers shine.

"Have you ever been beaten for your birthplace?"

But he just stares at me, like a bellboy without a tip.

***

I go home. "Wife," I ask. "What is the square root of decency?"

Wife laughs. "I could give you a calculation," she says, "but I'd rather give you an example." She pulls out the last census.

"I see there are more people than animals," I say.

"There are more animals than decency," Wife says.

"What does that mean?"

Wife puts a napkin on our cat. "Stay," she says, then:

"Let me explain. We crossed the sea, buried eagles in trash, chopped trees into houses, fed rivers to pipes. Now lakes are packed with asphalt. Fishes drink dirt."

"What's that got to do with me?" I ask. "I can count birds."

"Indians," she says.

Suddenly I'm lost in a dense forest of tall questions. All I thought true is covered in decay. My wife has betrayed me. My face is old.

"Let's eat a corn," I say. "That should help." My world is garbled.

"Your logic," my very own wife says, "is not welcome here."

Now I'm further dulled. I believed I was always welcome. I arrived with a thousand ships in my throat, coughed them across a continent. They skidded over mountains and prairies, discharging cities and sewage in their wake. Our culture took root and made the grass wither.

We always promised a better life. More secure, wealthier. Fewer slaves. Some explosions to shape the land, sure, a small price for large ambitions. We would reach the other sea, tame the savage hills, and fill the valleys with hot dogs and banjo music.

Wife pulls a knife from her robes. "Would you have me slice?"

Depends on what she wants to cut, I think, but I play along. "Why not?" I reply.

The knife loosens old dirt we had hidden. A landslide falls upon our relationship. A century goes by. She digs herself out. "Look who I found," she says. Chief stands by her side covered in welts and scars.

"Welcome," he says. "I have tried so long to reach you."

"You missed me by a hundred years," I say. "All my words flew to the burial grounds. I'm no longer the same."

"None of us are," says Chief.

Wife jumps up. "Give him a chance," she says.

Yes. I may have opposed justice while I slept.

***

Reporters knock the door, barge in. "What do you think of crimes against humanity?" they ask.

"They belong punished," I say.

"What about genocide? Forced relocation?"

"That must never happen again."

But the lips on TV that night aren't my own. They're lips exhumed from graves of ancestors who harvested riches with death marches and massacres.

"He agrees with us," reporters crackle. "Oppression is necessary. Plus, people love life in the ghetto. It's quite edgy."

"Turn it off," Wife says. "Deceit makes my stomach burn."

She's right. A slop trough of lies.

The screen fades and I hobble to the bedroom. Time to rest and in the morning take out the trash.

***

"Good morning Chief," I say. "What's the plan?"

"New plan," says Chief. He has clean on his shoes.

"What is it?"

"It's time you called me human," he says.

Agreed. It's overdue. And everybody else we've paved over.

"Yes," I say. "Let's do it right this time."

The bus pulls up to the curb. Before I board, I glance around. Towers that house the workers stretch into the smoggy bosom of the sky. Boulevards that spread our spawn form crisscrossed festered wounds filled with red lights and strip malls.

The driver holds the wheel with one hand and beckons me to enter with the other.

Last chance, his simple sign language says. Let's go. This is our very last chance.

THE CANYON

For three days it rained and everything he carried except for matches wrapped in oilcloth and tinned coffee got wet. His hat. Pack. Clothes. His boots. He ate cold beans and raw trout. When he looked up he saw the rim of the canyon far above. An unreachable border between worlds. What wilderness lay beyond and what civilization far beyond that had no relation to his presence inside the magnificent greatdeep fissure that split the demanding earth. He had entered the canyon weeks before at its wide and shallow sloped entrance where desert ended and mountains began their ascent. Now enclosed within its transcendent walls and alone with his past he hiked forever upriver. Impelled by a severe and nameless purpose.

Escape or excursion he couldn't say. Or wouldn't. Either way, only the canyon knew him. Only the canyon received him and it spoke a tongue he had yet to master. At night the river current revealed stories that had no ending. Only constant shifting. Flowing. A direction of epochs carved.

The rain stopped. He laid his clothes on rocks and in thrall of midmorning light sat naked while damp yielded to sunlight. He dressed, make a small fire and heated coffee. Strained through a washcloth as his father had taught him.

They had been here many years before. When he was a boy and his father for a brief time a protector. They hadn't penetrated this far into the canyon but they had entered at night with rain and mud and lightning. And a story of a man who had been boltstruck and died.

He still wondered what that would be like. To be sudden pierced by god's brilliant wrath in the darkness and transported at once to another realm. A rare encounter. Divine.

For weeks he hiked deeper into the motherhood of the mountains. A willing prisoner inside the great walls that led ever closer to the river's birthpools. Secreted in far tributaries and snowpacks.

Ancient granite slabs rose from the riverbed and steep climbed to the sky. In some narrow places vertical and emerging from the constrained and enraged current itself. No path along a bank at all. He entered the water and waded chest deep upriver clinging to crevices in the drenched wallrock. Each step a careful calculation. A blind reckoning with his forward boot in the hurtling water to find a submerged foothold. After came drying and a thanking that the canyon had granted him passage.

One day he came to an easing, a widening of meadow and trees. The water relaxed and rippled. He made camp and at night allowed stars in the canyon gap above him to bless their light down onto his face. At times he cried alone in the canyon's well for even the rationed view of the sky showed the expansive promise of the world. Made more glorious by its boundaries.

He rested for two days, fished. Drank his coffee. Received riversong into his need to let go his past. Honored in silence a sanctuary of solitude deep in the mountains. His body as soul in flight.

On the third morning he awoke in faint dawnlight to the rough odor of primitive breath. A large black bear sniffed his face. His hands at his side he exhaled softly and trusted the bear would sense that no threat stemmed from his prone figure.

He held only wonder that beast and man should meet at the bottom of the world and share a sunrise.

Afternoons came early in the deep. When the sun dropped over the western rim, shadows crawled up the walls to meet the embrace of night. Still time to tramp the canyon and climb over rock but conditions could quick change dangerous. Once in late afternoon he had tried to cross to the other side of the river in leaps from rock to rock but darkness caught him in the middle on a large slab unable to see the next leap and he slept that night with rivermist and rumble of swift current.

An assortment of slowpass days. At times rough going. The river vigorous and rapid. His other life far behind.

One night he dreamed he stood near the canyon rim and heard a deep voice call out from the abyss. The youth will war me, it said. He shivered and moved closer to the edge. Barefoot on sharp rocks. He cried a single tear and the canyon filled with sadness. A second tear and it filled with joy. He awoke. A soft heaven light burned in the air.

Next day midmorning a jumbled slide of large granite blocks choked the riverside. A wallslab had fallen and shattered ages before. It extended upriver about three hundred meters. An unstable hazardous passage made more perilous by the uncountable number of rattlesnakes that crowded the rocks to warm their coldblood in the morning sun.

He tucked his pants in his boots, laced them tight, found a stick and began the crossing. His route anfractuous and precarious as rocks tipped and threatened his balance. Snakebite maybe survivable, but to break a leg certainly fatal. Two hundred impossible miles back and an unknown distance forward. He edged ahead. Cautious. Fully alive. Aware of his choice. The snakes hissed and rattled. The sun ascended, an hour crept. Once past he laid down his stick, walked a ways, sat on a rock and breathed. Asked himself in silence why he hadn't waded the river and in silence answered trial. And trust.

He entered the current and knelt, lifted his eyes to the rim. The water marked his chest and for a moment he felt himself purified, cleansed. Maybe now named. He heard meaning in the canyon sounds and within the river's urgent rush. He spoke his first words. We all submit to loss, he said to the walls. Man or god. But we go on. He rose and dripped. Took a long breath. Looked ahead. The cradle of the canyon's birthplace yet upward.

BAZ TRIES CRIME FIRST TIME

A 10 p.m. streetlight cracks through the store window, casts mirrored letters on the floor, shines the shoes of three old strangers in line with a bag of chips or a bottle of seltzer for a Thursday night of bingo or some other senior fun when the bell above the door sounds and Baz Osborne, tall with 19 short years of life enters. He carries a gun.

"Everyone down," he says, waves the gun in the air. "Please."

Erkin Polat, owner and night shift clerk with a cloudy beard, starts to drop.

"Not you," says Baz.

Marcus Benson, second in line, retired parole officer, speaks up. "Just a minute, young man. I've got a bad back. I can't get down on the floor."

"Me too," says the guy behind him. He wiggles his cane for emphasis.

"What's with you guys?" asks Baz. He lowers the gun, but points it at the cooler.

Marcus looks around at his companions in line. "We're old," he says.

"Okay, you can stand there. But don't move please."

"What about me?" asks Erkin. "I'm not so young, either."

"I said not you."

"But I usually sit on my stool. My feet are killing me."

"Okay, okay, sit on it. Now give me the money."

Erkin sits, but doesn't reach for the register. "Why?" he asks.

"Are you stupid? Why do you think?" Baz takes a step towards the counter.

"Hey don't call me names."

"Oh, sorry," says Baz. "Sometimes I get stressed."

"That's okay," says Marcus. "Isn't that okay, Mr. Clerk?" Erkin nods. Marcus turns back to Baz. "What's your name young man?"

"Baz," says Baz. "But not really," he adds. His nose is sweaty.

"Okay Baz But Not Really," says Marcus, "Why don't you tell us why you want the money?"

Baz hesitates like he wants to say something, opens his mouth, closes it.

Shirley Doyle, first in line, last to speak, raises her arms with her palms flat. Her Coke waits on the counter. "Can we get this over with? It's getting close to my bedtime."

"Is that thing loaded?" asks the guy behind Marcus. He uses his cane to point.

"I don't know," says Baz. He lowers the gun to his side.

Shirley pivots. "You don't know?" She squints and puckers her lips like she can't believe an umbrella is leaking.

Baz turns a light shade of red and explains in a tenor of faint bravado that he doesn't know whether the gun is loaded because he doesn't know much about guns, in fact nothing at all really, but he watches TV and assumes that they're always loaded because that's the way it works on the screen and besides he's desperate.

"I was desperate back in 68," says the guy with the cane. "My platoon was trapped, just about wiped out."

"That's a shame," says Baz. "I'm glad you're okay, though."

"Christ. Shall we put some chairs in a circle?" asks Erkin. Marcus and Shirley exchange a glance, shrug.

"No, I guess this wasn't a good idea," says Baz. "I better get going."

"Where?"

"I don't know. My mom is sick."

"Home, then," says Marcus. "Go be with her."

"She needs medicine."

"There's a Walgreens three blocks over," says Erkin.

"They want money," says Baz.

"Don't they all," says the guy with the cane. He hobbles to the counter, lays his bag of nuts down. "I don't need these," he says, then pulls his wallet from his coat, removes 2 twenties. "Take it," he says to Baz. He looks around.

Shirley cracks a crust of makeup with one eye, fishes in her purse. "All right, I'll chip in," she says. Marcus digs in his pocket, follows suit.

"Not me," says Erkin. "I'm barely making a living here."

The guy with the cane taps it on the floor. "Come on man. You can afford it. You charge $6 for like three ounces of nuts."

"Okay, okay, but only 10 bucks." He opens the register, looks at Baz. "But leave the gun here."

Baz nods, sets the gun on a rack with potato chips. "Okay."

"And call me sir," says Erkin.

"Yes, sir."

"Now get out of here."

The bell above the door sounds. Footsteps fade on the sidewalk. The streetlight grows a little brighter.

ARMCHAIRS OF THE SWOLLEN SKY

The sun near the river cooled itself in the setting and we climbed down from our family of horses to observe heaven's descent. Our time fueled itself brief and we drove all our leftover doubts about the world's disorder as stakes into the sacrificial ground. It would do no good to worry. Outside forces would continue without us, and everything that we could do would only serve to create a future we could not yet see.

But we could imagine and build. And so we left our fears pinned as moths on the collector's cork.

One man near climbed from a bed of sorrow, considered us wrongheaded, and prayed that our uncertainties should rise and fill the air with their clamors, but as a single voice we told him to return to his yard of scattered graves from which he had surfaced and seek solace in his suspicion alone.

Months passed. We magnified our perception.

From the west a merchant ship appeared and from its holds spilled a thousand pieces of advice on everything from courtship to paragraph construction. But it all gusted over our heads and disappeared into clouds that rested upon armchairs of the swollen sky sharing secrets with the wind.

The vendors sailed away, and for this we lit twilight candles and bowed our thanks.

Ours was not an imitation life. Ours lay cast by forges made of iron years and by conflicts made of words that refused to die. If a man or a woman called out in the afterbirth of agony for that which had escaped our journey – those attachments of wealth, power, and our shield of righteousness we had tightclutched so long – we as one ascended the tallest tree and reminded our brothers and our sisters that these phantom concepts in the end provide no comfort, only a singular longing for more.

Our scars healed, our burnings cured, we returned to the land where we had started our pilgrimage to seek our families and friends. They too had been left behind.

They wore shock on their dark faces as if we had climbed from tombs of dynasties covered in the dust of our heritage. And perhaps we had. Perhaps we had followed footsteps of giants and having been vulnerable in their enormous world, given up the pretense that we were more than fleeting beings, trapped between grass and sky, beings that must make the best of each storm, each birth, and each passing.

For these educations we paid many prices but the greatest, and the most freely spent, was our loss of pride. Nothing exceeded the joy of our ability to see ourselves in others, to suffer the same setbacks and celebrate the same delights.

In time a day will rise from behind the hills when others will join hands with these values. We shall eat fresh fruit together and paint our days with suns that spill over rivers in the mornings and tip the forests into a barrel of night when the hour grows old. There we'll sleep and awake refreshed with a plenitude of family and food, and from our admixture create a new collective of human that is kind and wonderful and wise.

DUTY TO CONCEIVE

Laura stood in the kitchen, stared out at the neat rows of brown houses.

Morning. Gray sky. A knock on the door.

"Yes?"

"Sign here." A clipboard. A letter.

She closed the door, held the letter, looked at the sender, set the letter on the table, went back to the kitchen, stared out at the houses. A light rain fell.

The day moved across the sky. The gray remained.

At dinner, she told Paul. His face stayed stone. "We better read it," he said.

"Let's finish our food first." Two or three houses over, a dog barked.

They sat on the couch and read. Instructions from the Population Department. Brief and to the point. Child needed. Create one. As soon as possible. An agent will contact.

"What do we do?" asked Laura. She stared at the wall.

"We do what they say," said Paul.

"But I don't want to."

"The Department knows best."

"They don't know what's best for me."

Paul stood, paced, walked to a mirror on the wall, saw a tired, clean shaven man, massaged his cheeks, turned. "What do you mean?" he asked.

"I'll have to give it up, Paul."

"Maybe not."

"You know better than that."

"Yes," said Paul. "I guess I do." He sat again.

Rain dripped on the roof. On the street, a car passed, briefly illuminated the window.

"Maybe it won't happen," said Laura. "Maybe I won't..."

"What?"

"Conceive."

"Well, we have to try." He reached out his hand.

Laura stayed still. "Do we?" she asked. For a moment her mouth tensed, then fell.

"If we don't try, they'll..." Paul stopped, withdrew his hand, took a deep breath.

"I know."

A gust. Rain splattered the window

"Do you think I like this any more than you?" Paul asked.

"I think you don't care."

"I could lose my job."

Laura stood, backed away from the couch. "Your job?" she asked. Her forehead furrowed.

"We must live." Paul rubbed his temples with two fists, sighed.

"I hate this," said Laura.

"It's our duty."

Laura turned to face the window, the refracted street. "Do you love me?" she asked.

"Come sit," said Paul. He patted the couch.

She sat. "Answer the question, Paul."

"Yes, I love you. But our bodies are not our own."

"How did it come to this?"

Paul didn't answer. They held each other.

The rain intensified. It hammered the roof.

Hammered it more.

DAY OF THE BOMBING

Khary Bello at the boardinghouse window. Morning. Tattered side city. Scattered sky clouds. Small hunger. No voices. August.

Streetside, shoes cracked, he walked. Each day the same. Walk the old districts for a small job for a small coin. Sweep out a doorway. Throw a bag of trash in a pile of other bags of trash. Pity work for an old man, but he managed. On occasion thrived.

On the sidewalk a hatch opened in his mind and a voice dropped in that spoke in broken tiles and sparks from a bench grinder. It grated out the word *bomb* and Khary Bello put his hands to his head and whispered oh god.

He thought to tell a cop but he knew it was too late to save shattered victims they would deadlift from the rubble. It was too late for those who ran with redscream on their faces. The world coughed tragedy from its tainted lungs every dying day and Khary Bello was just one man. One man in a world of calamity.

The bomb had struck a hotel next to the park on the Avenue of Immortals. Khary Bello steered his feet in that direction to view the aftermath. A small spider of dread climbed his throat but he swallowed it down with the relief that death hadn't taken its shot at him this day.

Things not as he thought. Children chased a ball in the park and laughed. Taxis stopped at the hotel. Two women spoke calm. A cop leaned on a wall.

Where is the bomb? Khary Bello asked the cop and the cop said what bomb? The one I heard. No bomb here, beat it. The hotel bomb. Are you okay old man? I'm fine, said Khary Bello and the cop said then beat it. The world coughed up unwell people every dying day and the cop saw Khary Bello as just another glob of the sickness.

Black and white not the same as color, said Khary Bello and walked away.

He knew what he meant even if cops did not. Cops spoke only the language of rules and not of imagination or of ancestor voices and shared humanity. Khary Bello spoke of things both past and yet to come. A rainbow of possibility, a continuum.

Later they would examine another spilled casket of anguish and then wish they had heeded an old man with broken shoes. But he left the thought of future victims beneath the stained blankets of his belief and continued. He helped move a few boxes in the garment district, and with the coins he earned bought a bowl of soup and bread.

That night he lay awake in his cheap room with a warm breeze through the window and waited for a hatch to open in his mind but only silence. The curtain fluttered.

Next day the city wept for the bombing that killed woman and men and children and bellboys and cops in the hotel next to the park on the Avenue of Immortals but Khary Bello said nothing to anyone. Even if authority did open their ears to his prescience they would likely consider him perpetrator with an awakened conscience rather than oracle. Besides, he couldn't say how it worked. Voices cracked open his mind on their schedule, not his. And sometimes they merely muttered. Babylon.

That's how it was for Khary Bello. Lost. An inauspicious visionary. Chaotic. An unknown presence in a world that coughed out anonymous faces every dying day. Streetside, shoes cracked, he walked, looked for a job of no consequence. He low circled the mournful city for a small coin.

THE LONG IMPRISONMENT OF DAVID ROBERT JONES

When he was born, shortly after doctors examined him and determined that he was healthy and whole, he was assigned the identification David Robert Jones and transported to a nearby infant prison where the wardens placed him in a cell, covered him with a blanket, closed the door, and monitored his behavior from another part of the facility with surveillance cameras.

For the first several months of his imprisonment, David Robert mostly stayed confined to quarters. Although his needs were always met, at times he sensed a faint embryonic stirring to escape his captivity.

Naturally he couldn't articulate his desires except in primitive, instinctive wails, complaints which usually summoned one of the wardens who then sought to quiet him with indecipherable assurances that all the constraints were for his own good, and that one day his term would expire and he would be set free. Of course, as in all infant prisons, the wardens understood well the importance of keeping their prisoner pacified. But they themselves, having lived in various penitentiaries and reformatories of their own through the decades, knew that their promises were false.

One day near the end of his first year of incarceration, after much persistent urging of his custodians, David Robert Jones stood on wobbly legs, extended his arms, and spoke his first words.

Help me, he said.

Eventually David Robert was allowed time each day in the exercise yard to feel the sun on his forehead and gaze beyond the tall chain link where concrete corridors ran between one child detention center and another. As the first few years of his life extended their branches and David Robert grew, he was permitted to visit other children in other exercise yards, but always accompanied by a guard, and only when the stars cloaked themselves in daylight. At night he stayed closed in his cell.

When he was about six years old, David Robert Jones began near daily excursions to a nearby internment camp guarded by men and women with heavy books. They spoke the language of directives and proclamations. They moralized math, and articulated several overlapping philosophies that upheld the societal benefits of compliance. Also, as the blood wardens before them had done, they quieted any restlessness that arose with promises, by now decipherable, that the prisoners would one day complete their sentence and be at liberty to leave.

When a dozen years had passed, his fundamental habilitation complete, David Robert Jones was at last released into the larger surrounding prison made of countries and cities that contained larger, more luxurious cells.

With new choices of detention now available, David Robert entered the offices of an insurance company where he was assigned a job stamping papers with a kind of secular fisherman's ring. For years he sat in his cubicle and stamped.

What do you think? asked a coworker one day, and David Robert paused for a moment before answering.

Help me, he said.

As may happen at times, his plea managed to tap the bars of the prisoner confined to the other skull. The coworker, who introduced herself as Maria Ella, told David Robert to meet her after work where she would share a plan for escape.

They met in a small cafe, and Maria Ella told David Robert of the breakout planned for the following week. According to arrangements, prisoners from at least fifty other workplaces across the city would step from their cages in chorus and take to the streets to demand the keys to their own lives.

Like many, David Robert was unconvinced that escape from the penal routine was possible, but he was willing to try.

Pain is the decisive element of existence, he said.

Yes, said Maria Ella. It pushes us to pleasure.

The next week, a thousand men and women joined hands to celebrate the death of their internment and the birth of their liberation. They marched and called for the board of directors to conceive each life of each prisoner sovereign. At first it seemed to be going well, but soon correction officers rushed from their barracks. The uprising was quelled.

For the next several years, David Robert Jones wandered from one penitentiary to another, looking for one with fewer walls. In one rural town, far from the larger confinement complexes, he worked in a hardware store, but after several months realized he was still interned in a tight cell. The walls that pressed him weren't made of concrete or sheetrock, but rather a growing sense that there had to be more to existence than the pursuit of its continuation.

On a city street one day, an old man with craters on his face where eyes usually gathered tapped David Robert Jones with his cane.

They say that color is beautiful, he said.

They say the same of freedom, said David Robert.

We all suffer something, said the old man.

With this short exchange, David Robert understood that freedom needs a prison much like hope needs a despair. Uncertain of the implications, but heeding the urge to follow this realization back to its lair, he quit the city and climbed into a remote highland that looked out over the distant plains of penal colonies which lay flattened by perspective in all their incomprehensible multitude.

And there as hermit he stayed, far from the customary incarceration of civilization. He ate squirrels and pinenuts. He drank lakes.

But despite his solitude and contemplation, David Robert Jones still served his rooted habit of internment. It lingered like the smolder of bound bodies at the stake. Some perimeter of the world itself still fenced him. Emancipation had yet to remove its shackles.

Slow years passed. He searched the wilds for answers. He survived.

More slow years passed. He searched and survived more. His shadow grew smaller. His face sprouted old.

While fetching water one day, he slipped on a rock. As he lay with the pain, he realized that not only the world had constraints. His body advanced them, too. It was a fleshy prison of its own. Wherever he went, he carried his own limitations.

After a few minutes, he stood and limped forward to dip his bucket, slightly changed. He knew he had time yet to discover the freedom he had always sought, but he also understood that as his physical pace slowed and stumbled, time in opposition ran its own clockworks faster for the finish line.

One morning, the final of his imprisonment, David Robert Jones stood on the edge of his last opportunity for pronouncement, and wondered aloud, as he had read long ago, if all truths and wisdom were compressed into an indistinguishable moment of time as one stepped over the threshold of the invisible.

At his feet, an immense waterfall plunged to far churning pools. For David Robert, it seemed to fall from the height of his disquietude to a distant ethereal accomplishment of his quest. In its descent, it gave rise to a set of unsettling and yet oddly comforting thoughts.

If this precipice before him were indeed the last prison wall, freedom needed but one more leap. And yet maybe he, an old man born to the servitude of expectations and grown to the servitude of irresolvable pursuits, was at once both prison and prisoner. As jailer then, he alone could grant himself pardon.

For several minutes, David Robert Jones stood unmoving as the mounting sun warmed his hands and saturated his vision. An element of visceral knowledge stirred within him, and a long obstructed understanding ascended through the hollows of his bones. After a lifetime of forced and false roads, a simple route of escape lay within his reach after all.

DESTRUCTIVE EFFECTS OF IRRATIONAL BELIEFS ON A MOTHER'S SPINE

At times, beneath the lunar inception of night, when old memories, sharp and serrated, slice his serenity, Enrique Roberto Lopez Sandia recalls when he was a child on his way with his parents to the old country and how he wondered why one country should be old and another not so old and how his parents had little tolerance for his nascent peculiarities and so threw from their mouths repelling spears of words like: because I said so. And: one day you'll understand.

In the harsh fluorescence of the airport terminal Enrique had crossed a threshold with his left foot first instead of his right and knew that a majestic misfortune would soon slide from the skies in retribution for his error, for he had read the great Book of Fates and had acquainted himself with all the reckonings that stalked a life. He knew how they stood ready to strike like a phalanx of hostile intendants if the unaware or careless should stray from the cautious path.

He ran back into the night and the family missed their flight with many curses and clumsy suitcases and it wasn't until they arrived at their destination on another flight that they discovered that the first plane had nose dived into the Atlantic.

On this particular night, many years removed from his childhood, Enrique sat in his armchair and pondered his latest blunder. He had forgotten to hide his thumbs in his pocket when the bus he had been riding passed a graveyard.

Someone was sure to die. Someone close and filled with light and life soon to be skinshaved down to the pith where the fatal parts of existence dwell in harmony with their purpose, but where most people are reluctant to go.

You could not tell Enrique Roberto Lopez Sandia that the devil didn't live in two mirrors or that it was okay if a broom touched your feet. He had seen in fog and in clear air how all superstition gave birth to itself from the hot phosphorus of fact. A guy walks under a ladder and falls into a pit. A woman whistles inside the house and seven demons, in the shape of foul horses, force feed her a galloping illness.

Enrique slow slipped from his chair like a thick quilt and walked into the kitchen, his toes clenched against his shoesoles, and whispered my god.

I hear them, he said to himself. I see them dimly through cracks. Their voices aren't yet dead and yet already I am culpable, liable in the eyes of the Book of Fates and in the judgment of my peers.

It was an odd thought, even if only spoken to himself, because Enrique Roberto Lopez Sandia had no peers. He lived without a future or a wife, his principal companion a desert caravan of tortoise days.

You could eat his life straight from the sack, wash it down with orange juice and gin. You could rub his skin with salt. You could make noodles of his hair.

You could, but you wouldn't.

Dare.

Enrique did have a single friend, Marjorie Green, who lived in an trailer in a parking lot at the allnight supermarket where she collected beer bottles and broke them on the pavement whenever an errant dawn moon provoked her rage. Even a pink and songful emergence of sunrise caused choleric sandstorms to rasp her mood into rough splintered barnwall.

A woman of anger and crepitation. A man with god in the Book of Fates.

Their breasts hung slack, bathrobes in tatters. But they were faithful adherents. Enrique would never flip over a cooked fish because somewhere a ship goes belly up and dies like a cockroach in bleach, and for the same reason Marjorie would never wish a stranger good luck.

Despite their fixations, or perhaps because of them, they had become lovers, not of flesh that rotblacks if one places bread upside down in its basket, but platonic amorists united in their belief that the rest of the ignorant world poured bottled blindness in their eyes to shield themselves from the outrages and dangers that sat upon each architectural cornerstone like neoplastic gargoyles.

And in this union they were happy.

Not the happiness of cheer but that of belonging.

Their fixations grew from the same soil.

Watered by the same rank well.

On this particular night, many years removed from his childhood, Enrique walked to the trailer of Marjorie Green and tapped the aluminum door with three fingers, both to announce his desire to enter and to plead the Book of Fates a commutation of his recent bad blessing.

Inside, they gazed through curtain cracks that, like their concrete cousins on sidewalks, could split the spine of a mother or a daughter into three painful parts if the proper rituals were not respected. They watched shoppers enter the market and leave with their culinary wishes fulfilled, unaware that they could be the next child of tragedy, breech birthed from the womb of irrational beliefs or the maternal dredgeblade of anger.

They minded through the night and listened to the sounds of bloody slapping feet on wet pavement in the rain that carried gutters to culverts and culverts to the final necropolis of sea.

I wonder who dies this night, said Enrique, his voice chapped and cracked, and Marjorie replied that she was happy to see others suffer for her sins.

Silence. Late. The hour thin.

A time to push home past cab stands and hookers.

Time for another dark stage.

But Enrique and Marjorie rose, stretched their limbs into supple sheets, and walked out into the parking lot where they saw the rain dying in dawn and heard angled pale faces of the day's first luminescence affirm that a man is responsible for his mother's backbone, and to that end must never buy yellow flowers or eat bananas on a boat.

Shall we shake our black shirt? asked Marjorie.

No, said Enrique Roberto Lopez Sandia. I think we're safe for now. Marjorie sighed.

Safety.

Obsession.

Madness.

Each one leads to the other.

In ever diminishing circles. Cause and effect. Devoid of rhyme.

Each one gathers delusion and myth, seeks approval and sanction.

Waits.

Each one waits within the halls of its suffering for all the world's mothers, from Istanbul to Brisbane to the bloody ballrooms of Saint Petersburg, to strike their spines with headstones, make their paralysis public, and set their desperate and furious children free.

FAR BIRDS ABOVE THE AVENUE OF SAINTS

As a bird I would gently fly high above buses and those who mount sidewalks on a hardline damp day of waging war with office chores and bills to pay – but I'm a mere creature of arms and legs, and cannot reach an alien heaven from this Avenue of Saints. I'm stranded on the far shore of salvation.

On this street James and Julie and I are in the rain, our cardboard roof tapping the same slow hymn I remember from when I was a simple victim of family pain that thrust me from a home into the cold.

Once this city rested on a heart, but now it's broken and spent. Some few lucky grabbed a good life by the throat and squeezed it hard with their coffee delight and the freedom of another birthright. And oh, how they do fast-track their feet when they pass, never sleepless at night of what would happen should they not make the rent on time.

Once I prayed for a new start. Give me a new start, I said, my hands outstretched. Give me a job so I too can pay credit card fees and donate my spare spoils to charity. I'd like a handful of bills and guys at the door demanding payment. James and

Julie and I could tour from one encampment to another spelling the gospel of normalcy with our fingers, one united voice to the deafness.

It's just a dream. Most of my friends chase drugs down the alley and I must admit I too take needles in the arm and pills that stun the thought of the bond I once had with myself. For this habit I must steal into a store at night through a back door in Chinatown or the Guatemalan district, grab a handsome item to sell or trade for a burrito or a fix. But one day, tomorrow or the next for sure, I'll repair this broken timepiece inside me, watch the dials spin up another future.

Julie grabs me my the arm and shakes. "Wake up from your thoughts," she says. "The rain has stopped."

It's true. The outside rain. And I almost thank god.

Instead, we walk to the subway steps and ask the children of buses if they can spare a coin or a word of cheer for three souls who rose from the confines of confusion into the embrace of destitution.

We are the future, we cry. *We are you in ten years when your dreams collapse.*

Most continue their descent into the bowels of the city where the trains screech their rage and drag the crowds into their cage. On their breasts this nation wears crosses, but inside the marrow of bones it's all hammers and spikes.

That's what we see anyway, everyday the same, some providence, some rain. We can't climb from this divide, imprisoned in humanity's cracks.

In daylight, there's sky above the urban canyon and I see high gliding specks in my eyes.

But then night falls on my sight. I go blind to the freedom of flight.

LIFE AND DEATH OF ERNEST HEMINGWAY

When Ernest Hemingway killed himself with a shotgun in 1961 just shy of 62 years old, he did it because he saw the spiritual progression of those two numbers and because he had too much success in life, said Marcus as we paused outside a barber shop on the Avenue of Saints just down from the cathedral.

I was trying to light a cigarette and almost dropped my matches. That's nuts, I said once I got the cigarette going. Who kills himself over success?

I'll tell you kid, said Marcus. A guy seriously wounded in the war. A man with four wives and two plane crashes to drink to.

More reason to live, I said.

To you maybe, said Marcus. But Hemingway saw his death coming later that year and wanted to show it who's boss.

The barber came out onto the sidewalk brushing loose hair off his pants with both hands. I heard that, he said, and I think you're both nuts. I shave fifteen heads a day and nobody ever mentions a god damn thing about Hemingway. He went back inside.

Marcus grinned and shook his head. Let's go, he said.

We moved off and I got to thinking. From what I knew, Hemingway went to Cuba to talk to Castro and seems they hit it off pretty well. He also sold quite a few books. He even went to Africa once or twice. To hunt lion I think.

You ever been to Africa, Marcus?

They shoved me in Fort Hood on the way to the war. Long time ago.

That's Texas.

The war?

No, the fort.

Marcus grunted. If you say so, he said.

At an intersection we waited for traffic to pass. The sun down smashed the sky. In their cars people looked like flies trapped in jars.

I'd rather be dead than successful, I said.

Marcus crunched his face. Come on kid, he said. You don't mean that.

How do you know?

That's just something people say instead of admitting defeat.

Are we defeated? I moved my foot to one side.

He didn't answer, just watched the stoplight paint its child green. We crossed. It wasn't what Hemingway did with his life that's important, said Marcus. It's what he didn't do.

How's that?

He didn't take the world for granted. Didn't let people tell him right and wrong.

How about you, Marcus? You let other people tell you right and wrong?

A man's got to live.

Marcus was old, nearly fifty. He'd probably die soon because that's what happens when you cross the fifty year line. And the rebel juice leaked out of him long ago. But he was still a good guy and a good hustler. One time we found a bottle of decent whiskey only a quarter empty and sold swigs down by bus station east.

I'm living by my rules, I said.

Yeah kid, said Marcus. And I suppose you eat elephant meat.

What's that got to do with it?

Hemingway. Brought them down himself. Watched those tons of flesh fall right onto his plate.

Well, I don't have a gun, I said. Or I would too.

Marcus blatted a skeptical warbled note. Look around, he said. This is the real world. A frying pan.

The world is what we make it, I said. When I was a kid, trains stopped nearby to pick up stuff the factories pushed out. I'd steal what I could and sell it to the junk man. My mama read me stories of faraway pirates and executive murder.

You're still a kid, said Marcus. And you're still here.

Not forever, I said. My cousin lives up by the border and he says there's lots of action.

What kind of action? Same as here, I guess. The same? Yeah. So when you leaving?

Soon, I said. Well, maybe soon. Just need to work a few more things.

Okay, kid.

We turned right on Constitution and angled across the street to the shady side. Found a bench. Took a seat. A street vendor pushed some junk in our face and we waved him off.

Marcus? I said.

Yeah?

Do we face eternity alone?

Marcus flicked a bug from his arm. Where'd you come up with that? he said.

Found it in Hemingway's shrapnel wounds, his bloody knee.

Marcus raised his eyebrows. I guess we do kid, he said. We face it alone.

I'm not ready, I said.

Jesus kid, stop it. You've got your whole life yet.

Yeah, but I wonder what we're doing and why we're doing it. I don't even know how to get to Cuba.

Got a Hemingway urge? said Marcus. Maybe, I said. Well, at least you don't have a gun.

That's not funny, Marcus.

He stood. You're right, kid. It's not. A bus passed, belched black smoke.

Then what do we do?

Face it with dignity, kid. Courage and dignity like Hemingway said.

But he was talking about death, I said.

And you kid?

I got to my feet, looked around. I guess I'm talking about life, I said.

Same thing, said Marcus.

Same thing?

Yeah kid. Just a different colored hat.

A WORLD OF NO WHITE PAINT

Tuesday. Hollis Jenkins walked to the mailbox. Never a letter, but he had to clean out the junk every damn day. If not, some kid would pull it out and throw it in the street. Because he could. Mean or unpleasant or merely bored. A world of because they could.

Hollis had no affection for the outside world. Only a fierce defensive duty for his house and property. A government pension bought him beer and meat. And ammo. Beyond that, for all Hollis Jenkins cared, the world could bathe in its cesspits.

Hey Hollis, said a neighbor and Hollis turned away with his junkmail in hand to go to the house. No advantage in polite. Hell with them. A world of to hell with them.

Inside the TV told him to hate most everything and he said yes. A lot to get riled about these days. People stole catalytic converters and sheets of plywood. Lightbulbs. Jobs. Culture. They even drained the blood of language so that words no longer took sides.

A knock on the door. Gun on the table.

What do you want?

Campaigning for Daniel French, sir.

I hate the French.

It's his name, sir. He's not really French.

What's he want? To be our next president, sir. Will he get rid of Mexicans?

What?

Never mind, said Hollis. Get out of here. He shut the door. Walked back to the living room. Set the gun back on the table.

Wednesday. Hollis walked to the mailbox. Never a letter, but he had to clean out the junk every day. No consideration. Hey Hollis, said a neighbor.

What do you want?

We've having a barbeque on Saturday.

So? Thought you might like to come. Why? Because we're neighbors I guess.

Free beer?

Jesus, Hollis. What's with you?

Not a damn thing. A world of not a damn thing. Hollis went back inside and considered more fear and hate. His gun watched over him.

Thursday. Hollis walked to the mailbox and spat in the street.

Thursday night. The TV told Hollis to fear everything except white paint and Hollis said yes. Can't be too careful. A world of pitfalls and traps. Everyone out to gut you.

Headlights invaded the window and Hollis grabbed his gun and went outside. A dark car with three kids in it.

What are you doing? said Hollis. He knocked the glass. Roll down the window.

Driver kid. Dark complexion. Light beard. Maybe twenty. Twenty five. Border south.

Well? said Hollis.

Nothing, said Driver Kid. Wrong house I guess.

Stand my ground, said Hollis.

What?

That's what I say when the cops put a sheet on you. You're trespassing.

Fuck, you're crazy. Calm boat please. We're leaving.

Hollis showed his gun. Don't you call me crazy, he said. And he meant it. He wasn't. He was just a guy with an altogether normal worry that he might not make it to next week before an extremist with a random grudge took him out. Or some derelict trespassing thief would steal his proud place in the world. Or the flag would turn black. Or one day he'd wake up to find his neighborhood sold houses to anyone. Or the country would get so swarmed with dark skin that he'd have to go to the back of the line at the grocery store. Or the rivers would fill up with waterlogged bodies of children who couldn't make the swim from the third world and that their family behind them would use them as stepping stones so they could set up food trucks and force Hollis to eat their spicy food. Or one day he'd find the gun store closed, out of business. Or they'd outlaw white paint.

Driver Kid moved the shift to reverse. Stop, said Hollis. He pushed his gun through the window.

Whoa Abuelo, said Driver Kid. I told you we're leaving.

Apologize.

For what?

Coming on my property.

Okay, okay. Sorry. It was a mistake.

No mistake son. Get out of the car.

Why? And Hollis said because I've got the gun and Driver Kid shiftpushed the transmission to Park and got out. A thin ugly moon tangled a tree.

Why do they put the words *New Image* on tubs of cottage cheese? said Hollis.

What? You heard me. I don't know. Why? I don't know Abuelo, said Driver Kid. And his eyes said crazy alright.

It was a good question. At least Hollis thought so. If you didn't know the brand, you wouldn't know it was a new image. If you knew the brand enough to realize it had a new image, you wouldn't need to be told. If you knew the brand but not enough to know it had a new image, which had to be just about everybody, you wouldn't give a shit.

Answer the question kid, said Hollis. Driver Kid looked over at his friends, but they were silent. Hey, said Driver Kid, help me out here, but his friends looked like alumni of mute school. Afraid or inept or merely dumbstruck. A world of silent companions.

Look mister, said Driver Kid.

Okay, forget that one, said Hollis. Answer this. What's the best paint?

Are you okay?

Hollis pushed the gun against Driver Kid's chest. I'm fine, he said. What's the best paint?

Dutch Boy?

No. The best color.

Oh, said Driver Kid. He looked around. The streetlights cast cones.

White?

You're not sure?

Look mister, we didn't mean nothing.

Anything. What? You didn't mean anything. What? Double negatives, son. What?

Christ what is wrong with you? said Hollis Jenkins. I ought to let you have it right now. Right here and right now and call the cops and tell them you came to molest me and they'd say good job my man. Our gratitude. I could get your buddies, too. Tell them it was hoodies made me do it.

Jesus, said Driver Kid.

Ah, you're scared of me, said Hollis. He lowered the gun. That's good. And important. That people know I'm not just some fanatical old guy with cheap beer and regrets and guns and no friends. That what you think?

No, no. I don't think that.

Then what?

Look mister, I don't know.

Forget it, said Hollis. I know who I am. He tucked the gun back in his pants. Go on. Get out of here before I change my mind. And get that goddamn car painted white.

Driver Kid got back in. Closed the door. Put it in reverse and backed out with a groan of old shocks as he braked on the street and slammed the car into forward. The kids soon disappeared. A dog barked.

Hollis went back inside. Set the gun down and opened a beer. Sat by the chronic TV. Sighed. Put mental checkmarks on his list of virtues. It matched exactly his list of resolute doubts.

HIGH CAPACITY

After school one day, when my friend Ben asked me if I wanted to be a martyr, I said maybe. Truth is I didn't want to put my ignorance on display. I didn't know what the word meant. Whenever that happens, when my capacity is challenged, *maybe* is the best response. It lets you appear indifferent, and gives you a good excuse if you want to change your mind. *Sure*, you can say later. *Martyrs are okay. But not on Tuesday.*

Six years ago, when I was eleven, my father and I drove almost two hours from Grundy where we live to Abilene to see a rodeo. My mother had recently left us for another marriage. "Thomas," my father said with his arm out the window getting a light lopsided sunburn, "sometimes you need to kill what you love." I didn't know what he meant. My father said weird shit from time to time and I figure he was testing me to see if my capacity was filled up. In this case, a strong affirmative was in order.

"Yes sir," I said. "Sometimes you sure do."

I had learned long before that people don't actually care how you respond as long as you say or do *something*. I had enough capacity to know that I couldn't answer with nonsense like: *dog moon on barn roof*, but as long as the world thought you were paying attention, even a little bit, they just nodded and pushed out a self satisfied look, not because they thought you were in agreement, but because their voice was important and it had let their thoughts slip out through the bars of their mind.

Ben and I were working in the afternoons on Old Man John's farm, a bit out of town, cleaning up after cows and chickens. Old Man John had two sons, Big Nate and Taller Sam, but they went off to chase girls in Dallas, and Old Man was left with his bum leg and some thirty acres of poor land that didn't feed well and didn't grow well either. Old Man didn't pay much, but we didn't have any other prospects and West Texas without prospects is like fishing in a dry lake.

"Did you hear about Big Spring?" Ben asked me, after he had asked about martyr. We were out back with shovels and stink sweat. An old heifer rested on a patch of grass nearby.

Pretty sure he was still testing my capacity. I nodded. Nods are good, too. They're vague and they make it seem like you know what the other person is talking about. Also, and probably most important, the other person takes it as a signal to continue; they'll fill you in and you never have to reveal your ignorance.

"A guy there took a gun to school."

"Guns are good," I said. But I didn't really know for sure. Of course I knew something about them – everyone did – but I never had one before. No money, really. My father fixed cars, like a lot of people it seemed, but he wasn't particularly good at it. He was strong enough, could drop a transmission, but lacked capacity. Most people took their cars somewhere else, but once in a while some poor slob coming through town with a busted fan belt would see the sign out on the highway and in desperation pull in the driveway and up to the shop where my father sat, usually with a Budweiser in one hand and a crescent wrench in the other, looking like he had just got done reading a shop manual on *How To Fix A Buick In Your Spare Time*.

Ben tossed a shovel full of glop in the wheelbarrow. "Let's do it," he said.

"Do what?"

"Take a gun to school."

I said nothing, just rested my right foot on the shovel blade like a movie star tough guy in a movie about tough guys who square off and don't let the world tell them what to do. I didn't pull it off though. Ben looked at me funny, like I was something to be pitied, like I didn't have enough capacity.

***

Next week my mother died. I was surprised, not by the event, but by my reaction. I had thought sure that such news would be rendered insignificant by distance and time. After all, she had left seven years before, a few months after my brother Hank was killed, and gone to Amarillo to live with her new husband who wrote reports for an oil company. How many barrels this quarter, how many workers, that sort of thing. Before she left, she told my father she was tired of old tires and car parts.

"I'm tired," she said.

"Of what?" he had asked.

"Old tires and car parts."

I was in the kitchen at the time and the way she said it sounded like she didn't mean Goodyear or piston rods, but rather my father who had become those things and in doing so, become dirty and discarded himself, like junk you see on the side of the road.

The news came in a letter. *Dear Arthur*, it read. *I regret to inform you that my wife Margaret, your former wife and mother to your son Thomas, has expired from chronic obstructive pulmonary disease.* It went on about how wonderful she had been and how she was a light among lights, but that's what people say when somebody dies so they don't sound cruel even if they had hoped with all their heart that the person would hurry up and get off the planet. Signed: *Yours truly, Matthew Kinsman.*

Father set the letter down and sighed. We were on the porch, each in an old chair, with a small table in the middle, like two guys casually dividing up an estate, each with high capacity, each with the wits and the wherewithal to keep the other from taking advantage. "Are you okay?" he asked.

I wouldn't be tricked. He did this sort of thing before when I was twelve. Asked me if I was okay when Jesus, our Redbone Coonhound, died. I said no, I wanted him back, and my father hit me with the pick handle we were using to scape out a grave. I knew better – he was testing my capacity – and I had let down my guard.

"I'm fine," I said. But I wasn't. I was inside a volcano. The lava was far away, deep and asleep still, but I could hear it bubbling as it dreamed. I could smell smoke and charred bodies, faint like a fire in the next county. You can't see the flames or feel the heat yet, but you know the wind is bringing it closer. The wind is not your friend. It either brings bad tidings or takes away the sweet smell of pancakes a mother used to make. It takes her perfume and scatters it so that it's no longer special, no longer given to one boy and one boy only, but spread out and diluted among the ranch hands and storekeepers for a thousand miles until finally the sea takes it and feeds it to fishes.

***

I was nine when Hank went to Marine recruitment in Fort Worth and signed up. Since he was so much older than me, I used to think my parents had one kid, decided enough, cut the tubes, changed their mind years later, couldn't make a new baby, and then in a fit of providence found me abandoned under a rusty flatbed truck on the side of the road. I was probably dropped off by some drugged up lady on her way to California, left to die under the flatbed slats because that's what the world does when it sees you as weak or wobbly. Young or old, off you go to the trash heap if you can't pull your weight, if your capacity is damaged. Later, I realized that was not the case, that my parents had a little vasectomized miracle which was probably worse because that meant they hadn't ever wanted me in the first place.

About a year after Hank left, two Marine guys knocked on the door. I was in my room and saw them from the window. I couldn't hear what they said, but my mother fell down and my father put his fist through the living room sheetrock. The Marine guys got back in their car and drove off.

A few days later my mother took me aside. Although she wouldn't leave for Amarillo right away, I think she had already made up her mind. "He didn't protect him," she said. "He didn't protect me." She meant my father of course, and that's when I knew for sure I needed capacity. It had already been growing, but that was the moment I knew without a doubt that I would nurse it and make it strong. If father couldn't protect us from the world, that left me to do it. Someone had to stand up to the world. Someone needed to see the tears on my mother's face and say *that's not right*.

***

Two days after the letter from Amarillo, I met Ben behind the jail. We would go there to sneak smokes and listen for prisoner sounds. Although Ben and I were the same age, he was bigger. I could get on his shoulders and peek through the heavy meshed window to see if Sheriff Mason had captured a deadly convict on the run from the federals after escaping from a max security facility in Mississippi. Usually it was just a drunk cowboy, but I would still ask.

"Hey Mister," I'd say. "How many people you kill?"

Ben told me sorry about my mother and I said sorry about my mother too, but I didn't tell even him, maybe my only friend, that my nonchalance was an act I put on like boots. But instead of protecting my feet, my calmness protected my capacity. True I hadn't seen my mother for a long time, except for a visit now and then, but I could never forget how she threw me away like an old toy. When you're young, you can't do anything. The world shuts you out and leaves you losing and lost like it doesn't care if you live or die. It's full of kids from all corners bursting the towns into cities. You choke on the trash in the air until your breath is gone and your face is full of ants that climb from the sack of lies the world puts over your head. Only way out is capacity. You can't make it in the world without it. But they don't want the competition. They don't want new brains with new ideas ready to rapid fire them into the body of society and make it blow apart at the seams when it realizes how the past is a corpse and that they are now forced to face the grip of the future as it sprays itself in circles until all authority falls victim to the carnage that the future represents. They don't want that. They tell us what to do and what to think as if we won't someday replace them. They tell us we have no capacity when it's them who lack the determination to go into the mass of men and say: *it is time to die*, to get out of the way of the next generation who live inside brass shells and chew pieces of lead to show the world what they're made of. They're made of capacity, high capacity and yet the world would have us in institutions, confined to a ward until your viewport shrinks and all you have left is a coffin. All you have left is a grave to fall into with the masses who came to the festival of life and were slaughtered.

Ben prodded me. "Want a drag?" he asked. I took the smoke and sucked it hard into my lungs and let the nicotine spread its charms into body. For the moment, the world let me loose and I turned my head, as if looking at something up the street. I didn't want Ben to see that my eyes had become damp and shiny.

***

We heard about it the next day. Sherriff Mason was out by Ray Canyon near the South Wichita river when the call came in. "Breaker, breaker, one nine, come in," said Lois. Sometimes she liked to call herself dispatcher and pretend she was on TV, but Grundy, population maybe 4000, hardly needed a person dedicated to the radio. Lois made coffee, filed papers, answered the phone, and helped the sheriff when he needed something from the courthouse.

"Cut the crap Lois," said Mason. "What do you got?"

"Body over by the Pitchfork," she said.

"Shit," said the sheriff. "On my way."

Turns out it was just Old Better Paines, fallen down, passed out from too much whiskey like always. He'd been a fixture around Grundy forever and couldn't seem to go a week without getting dark drunk and making a mess out of himself. I felt kind of sorry for him and would even exchange a few words with him on a sober day, which were few, but Ben seemed to think that Better Paines deserved something other than pity. According to Ben, if you felt sorry for an old man who pissed his pants, the world would laugh at you for the weakling you show yourself to be.

"I would have taken him out," said Ben.

"What do you mean?" I asked.

"A bullet," he said. "The guy's useless."

Ben's likes to spout off fantastic shit sometimes because he thinks that people are impressed, but they're not. People are impressed by capacity, the capacity to keep your ideas to yourself so that people don't see you coming. Even if I agreed with Ben, I wouldn't say. Everybody in prison is there because they didn't have the capacity to make a plan and complete it without revealing themselves. You've got to be stealthy if you want to get by, sneak up and rapid fire your plan into the world, then slip back out before anybody knows what hit them, what struck them in the chest and toppled them like a human tree. They're stunned, too taken aback by the overwhelming intellect and precise execution of the man who pulls off the successful surprise to do anything but gasp for breath.

"*You're* useless," I said. "You're too transparent. People are going to hear you."

Ben laughed and hit my arm. "The famous ones always announce," he said.

***

That night my father was in a good mood. It happened once in a while after a good job that brought in a decent amount of cash and a decent amount of Budweiser that brought him to the brink of happiness without tipping him into a barrel of despair.

"Thomas," he said when I came up the driveway. "Sit with me."

We sat on the porch again, the table between us as it ought to be when two male bodies and two male minds want to be close enough to share but not so close as to offer the temptation of a hug. It was about six o'clock and the sky had the look of rain. The clouds were light gray in places, but contained several clumps of blackness that seemed like faces of kids who tried to escape from wherever they lived and find a new life as far away as possible but had instead been sucked up into the heavens where god said *too much salt* and spit them back out to scowl, sullen and hostile, at all the beautiful people below and to plot in the swirl of their cloud minds their kid revenge.

"You ever think about what you want to be when you grow up?" asked my father.

Even my father, once in a while, at times like these, wasn't testing my capacity. I could tell by the way his voice didn't hold a verdict in its tongue. It felt odd to see the world pleasant in these moments, but I imagined my capacity could use a short break once in a while. Like most things, it too needed to lay itself down every so often and nap.

"A doctor, maybe," I said. I didn't know how I was ever going to pay for doctor school, but the idea of helping people get well appealed to me. I could see myself with a stethoscope saying *that's okay, you're not going to die yet* and administering medicine with a giant syringe that I would jab into their flesh ever so gently so that their blood, which always waited for a chance to leap free into the air, would stay contained in its vessel.

My father didn't say anything, just looked out at the lowering sky with a thoughtful expression on his face, as if answers to all his questions of *why* hung there, ripe and ready to be plucked if you had the courage to stand up and stretch out your arm. That was the hard part sometimes. Not the questions, but the answers. Not the selections, but the choice. I knew sometimes people didn't like what they found.

"Or maybe a martyr," I said. Another trick I had learned. If the mood is right and you throw a small bit of uncertainty out to the world, it will grant you a small pardon.

"Do you know what a martyr is?" my father asked.

I confessed I didn't. I didn't tell him who had mentioned it. Father wasn't particularly fond of Ben, although to think about it, he wasn't particularly fond of anybody. He had his moments, like now, but mostly he saw the world as an unfriendly place.

"Jesus was a martyr," he said.

I thought he just dug holes and ran after squirrels until I realized my father meant bible Jesus, the guy with long hair who lived outside mostly and wanted to make money illegal.

"Yes," continued my father. "He died for his cause."

My capacity woke. I guess Jesus had a rough time too and went out to massacre Romans so they'd leave him alone and let him play with his friends without taxes and eat from the garden without a job. I imagine he too got fed up when people tested his capacity and told him he was a no good slacker. I bet he dug deep into the dirt of his heart with a stick and found the worms the world had planted there, discovered that the world wanted his heart eaten little by little, day by day, until it couldn't pump the life he wanted through his veins anymore. And so he snapped, went on a rampage to prove to them who was boss: who with the sheer strength of his capacity could shatter the doors they had closed to him; who could show all the teachers and priests and judges and cops that they had at last met their match in the never ending contest of wills; that he Jesus, son of man and son of no man, was nobody's fool and would mow them down with his peace gun so they would know at last what it was like to be an outcast, forever looking through a window at the happy dancers, forever painted with a dark brush because the world couldn't see his capacity, or if they could, wanted to quickly throw it into a pit and cover it with lime and pig shit so that it could never grow, never flourish into a flower or a tree that others would want to smell or taste. That's what the world does. It lives on a hill and never lets the beggars pass.

My father drank another beer and then went inside. I stayed on the porch for a long time watching the rain build. It came closer and closer and at last cried itself into the dust. It wasn't much. The promise held in the faces of blackness was not yet released. Their time would come. My time would come, too. If there's one thing that capacity tells you, it's that patience is a virtue. I learned this from my mother when I was seven. She said that although a chestnut, it was true. The only chestnuts I knew at the time were ones we ate once in a while, and that didn't seem to make sense, but I had said *thank you*. I believed I had understood enough to know she was trying her best to prepare me for the world. She wanted me to let the world in and not fear it, but even then there was a seed of distrust growing. It had barely sprouted and might never – even now – reach a height, but I could not then and cannot now ignore it. It's like a weed that should be pulled but has a sweet smell and so draws you near.

***

About a week later, I saw Julia Rodriquez over on Morrison Street by the supply house, although she didn't see me. She was a little bit older than me and was pretty but not too much so. Which was fine because otherwise I would have seen her as completely unapproachable instead of mostly so. She had dark eyes, dark skin, and a high perky nose that reminded me somehow of a rabbit. I used to think of her as my secret friend and had even invited her once to a movie, but I found out that there's no such thing as secret friends, only hidden enemies.

Several months before, when I had asked, she said she had to check with her parents and would let me know the next day. "Meet me at the drugstore," she said. I did. I sat outside on the bench there for twenty minutes past our appointed time when I saw her coming down the sidewalk with three of her friends. One of the girls giggled as she lifted her foot onto the entrance stoop of the store and I heard an alarm sounding inside the room in my head where I keep my fears guarded.

"Hi Thomas," said Julia.

"Hi."

She looked over her shoulder to see if her friends were watching, then turned back. "I can't go to the movies with you," she said.

"Yeah. Parents," I said. I tried to keep it casual, my capacity charged, because I sensed I needed a good shield, but my capacity seemed to be sluggish and woozy, like the best boxer had punched it in the face.

"No," she said. "My parents don't care. It's just that I want a boy who knows how to treat a woman and doesn't smell like old motor oil."

She'd been practicing that, I could tell. And it hurt. But it was the laughter that followed that opened my body up and crawled in. It was the overwhelming amusement that I had provided that chewed my ribs and ripped my stomach apart, piece by piece until I had nothing left inside but shells, sharp and empty of song. This is what the world does when your capacity is not plugged in. It grabs you and shakes your pockets until whatever meager coins of dignity you might have roll down the street toward the sewer. Nobody wants to rub you. Nobody wants to touch your hair, full of cobwebs and lice, matted with misery, awful with contempt and missing strands where you had pulled them from their roots in a desperate attempt to prove that your thoughts are clean. That *you* are clean. Nothing comes to your aid at these times but your capacity. It must be vigilant. Only it can pull you up, put you on your feet, rinse the world from your heart and leave you stronger, more capable, ever renewed and eager to hurl the world into a casket and nail shut the lid. Your capacity is your weapon; capacity is yours to command; it is your superior being that gives your life meaning when the world would swat you like flies on a window pane. I was in agony for maybe two weeks after Julia's joke, but I recovered. I came back from the edge of madness to stand resolute with my capacity. It would help me plan; it would help me plot. My capacity entered my empty spaces and filled them.

***

Ten o'clock at night in the park. Ben sat down. The iron bench had streaks of rust; the half moon gave it a deliberate look as if an artist schooled in deconstructivism instead of some slipshod town worker had done the work. Tomorrow was Saturday, but even if it had been a school night, my father had gone to bed and didn't much care if I stayed out. Ben's parents probably felt the same.

"There's a bus in an hour," said Ben. "Last one to Abilene."

"What's in Abilene?" I asked.

"Connection in the morning to San Angelo. Big parade there."

Ben could be like this. Wouldn't come and say something. Wanted me to summon my capacity and draw it out of him like well water.

"Come on Ben. What do you want?"

"I've got it," he said. "A whole duffel bag of them. All sizes. Bullets, too."

Ben's words went into my ears and flowed down the sides of my neck into my chest. I felt an excited tightening there. Sometimes dreams are just dreams, ideas are just thoughts. But sometimes dreams and ideas, coupled with capacity, can march out the door, ready for action. Mostly, the world wanted to stomp your dreams, whether dreams of doctor or martyr. World liked compliant soldiers that went forth in authorized, controlled encounters, and came back silent or not at all. World didn't like the unexpected interruption of routine. And what the world liked, capacity didn't. Capacity was to the world like a rock crusher to bricks. Something chimed in my head. A curtain slid back. We each snuck back home, grabbed our stuff, got down to the bus station and boarded.

***

At the bus terminal in Abilene, nobody gave us a second glance. With Dyess AFB nearby and Goodfellow further south, a traveler with a duffel bag was as common as an egg in a henhouse. We caught some sleep waiting for morning propped up by our arms on chairs, but this too was a common sight. From Abilene, San Angelo was another couple hours south.

Despite our normal appearance, a cop must have sniffed out my capacity. He probably didn't know what it was, just something slightly out of place like salad dressing on a hamburger.

"Morning boys," he said. It was about 7:30 a.m. "Everything okay?"

I'd done this before a hundred times. Trick is to hold your capacity down for a moment, let it see the world and guide you, but don't let it off the leash right now. Cops especially hate capacity, partially because of their training, but mostly because they don't understand it. If they understood, they wouldn't be cops.

"Yes sir," I said. "Just a little tired, but excited to be on our way to the oil fields." I put on just the right shade of smile and slack eye.

"Ridgefield?" the cop asked.

A trap, but I wasn't going in. Everyone knew Ridgefield wasn't hiring. Old man Ridgefield was a stingy bastard. "No sir, C&R," I said.

"Well, I hear they pay good," said the cop.

"Yes sir," I said. "We're going to save up for college."

That hooked him, got him to think about the good youth of today while any suspicion he might have had scampered off. Plus right then a woman on the other side of the terminal spilled coffee on her lap with a curse. Cop wished us luck and walked away.

***

As Ben and I traveled down highway 83 to San Angelo, the sound of the bus engine reminded me of the motor that powered the Ferris wheel at the county fair. It was the last time Hank took me there, right before he went off to a war I couldn't understand. Some older brothers can be mean, but not Hank. I had loved him, probably more than anybody, then or since. He tried to teach me that the world can be a good place. Although his efforts didn't stick too well, had things gone differently, they might have.

The Ferris wheel wasn't much as Ferris wheels go, but at nine years old, it seemed to have the capacity to take you high above life and give you a glimpse of a more exceptional sky. I was in line with Hank when two cowboys shoved me out of the way and cut in. I don't know if they didn't see Hank or they thought he wasn't with me, but they soon discovered their mistake.

The most remarkable thing about the incident was that Hank never once raised his hand, nor the volume of his voice, nor did he unleash his capacity. He used it, but kept it in check. His face changed, from someone who smiles at cotton candy to a stone hard warrior who doesn't care what weapon you hold. He seemed to grow taller. His voice changed too, from just another guy at the fair to a man who does not take no for an answer.

"Go to the back of the line," he said. "And don't touch my brother again."

Later we sat at the top of the wheel while they loaded passengers below. The fairgrounds were sprinkled with red and white lights and off in the distance, I imagined I could see the glow of Knox City.

"Thomas," said Hank. "Life is a beautiful painting."

He said things like that sometimes and I don't know where they came from. I never thought that way, but figured that maybe with his help I could someday. But two weeks later, he shipped out and was gone.

***

Ben and I walked into downtown San Angelo with the duffel bag. The parade hadn't started yet, but people were setting up folding chairs on the sidewalk and a few blocks away I could hear a marching band start up, halt, and start again as they performed a last minute tune up on their routine.

"I'm off for a final piss," said Ben. "Watch the bag." He wound his way through the crowd until his head bobbed behind a stop sign and was gone. It seemed he went off too quickly, but with the crowd getting bigger and my toes feeling tight, I was distracted and didn't consult my capacity.

Kids were running around everywhere and their parents didn't seem to care. Maybe they didn't. Maybe they secretly hoped that their offspring would leap into a hail of batons and be so consumed by the force that hit them that they would keep on death marching with the band right off the cliff of the world and lie there at the bottom, broken, liberated from their capacity. Maybe all the old people in the world wished that everybody younger than them would spin in wild pirouettes, shooting bright red punctured ribbons from the body of their future onto the street, when the final act came. Maybe everybody wanted everybody else gone because they couldn't face their own lack of capacity; they couldn't bear to look inside themselves and see the emptiness that stared back, unconcerned about right or wrong, indifferent to cries or pleas, distanced from the forces that drive men to commit actions considered unspeakable. But someone must say it. Someone must do it. Someone must strangle the world with its own birth cord.

Otherwise, we grow up, have more kids that suffer, and repeat ourselves in an endless cycle. The wheel that grinds us into dust can be broken. Once people see what we release on the world, the power of capacity, they'll come to their senses and stop the illness that wraps us in madness. They'll do the right thing and let capacity rule the world wisely and justly: for each child a place of dignity, for each mother a son who helps with the chores, for each brother another brother that spreads light and does not fade with the years into darkness.

* * *

Fifteen minutes later, the parade was about to start and Ben still hadn't returned. The doubt that nibbled at my resolve took a bigger bite. Two are stronger than one, but it seemed certain that Ben wasn't coming back. He must have looked his capacity in the eye and couldn't handle the sight reflected there. That's where people go wrong, even people you think are resilient and convincing. At a moment of truth, they get down in the dirt with their capacity, see it for what it is, and decide that it's too much for them. It looms too large with its bottomless gaze into the horrid depths of the human heart.

I was alone with the bag. It was just a bag, but at the same time it was much more than a bag. It was bigger than me and bigger than everyone who had come before me ready to let loose their capacity as great martyrs who never let go their cause. The bag and I were brothers, companions in a war that must boil over into the guilty streets. It was time to finish that war, correct the failure that was my life, a failure not my fault, but that of demons in the world that hated my capacity. How they hated. I gave them love and still they hated.

The bag had a long black heavy zipper that whispered when you slid it open. It had many stories it wanted to tell. The ones from Big Spring, Virginia Beach, Highlands Ranch, Orlando, Aberdeen, Las Vegas, Cincinnati, El Paso. All of them will pour out at once when I grasp the zipper pull between my thumb and forefinger. They will spill out and fill the air with shouts, with sounds of running feet, with the crack of wild precision that isn't a contradiction but rather the natural result of mixing rampage with capacity. Each person will make their own choice. Some will lean in, some out. In the end it only matters that you are true to yourself. Coward or hero. Servant or conqueror. A doctor or an assassin.

I don't know what I'll be remembered for, or if I'll be remembered at all. They say that great acts take great capacity, but sometimes I wonder if it's me or the world that has control. I could walk away, take a bus, study medicine, find a cure for chronic obstructive pulmonary disease. I could wait for the music to start. It's times like this I wish I had another hand to guide me.

THE CRYING GIRL

Morning breaks the window open, sets sunlight to shatter on the floor, the scorpions to scatter. They run for walls, but Jordan climbs from bed, his dream head raw, brooms them to the door.

A young boy appears, still untouched by caution, a child who never had a fall he couldn't master or a creature from which he couldn't run. His name is Ethan. He climbs in through the window when the sun creates the trees each day. "Good morning, Mr. Jordan," he says.

"Good morning Ethan. What do you do?"

"Same. I hear the girl that cries."

The house is large with a hundred halls. The girl that cries is never still for long, moves from room to room, from nook to cranny. Townsmen say she fell from a ship in the sky, but Jordan doesn't put legends in his mouth and chew. The island is full of tales and Jordan full of books and learning.

"It's just the wind, Ethan."

"Papa says wind is God and girl who cries his daughter."

Jordan pushes his teeth tight. The boy's father sailed into an cruel storm; he's not coming back. Ethan still wraps his heart in hope.

"Let's go to the kitchen," says Jordan. "We'll eat pineapple."

The island is blue with houses, and green with growth. From the kitchen they see sailcloth in the harbor, and at the edge of their world, the cerulean horizon.

Ethan puts a fork to his plate, lowers his mouth to table, sweeps the sweetness inside. "Where my Papa go?" he asks in between chews.

Jordan sees murky rocks and deep fish behind his eyes. "I don't know," he says. Every morning the same question, same innocent wonder, same lie.

"Let's ask crying girl."

They walk halls, open doors, ascend stairs. Wind carries the girl from place to place, always around a corner to the left, right, up, down into the secret deep, carved into island rock. House sits inside a larger house inside an even larger house, nested like facing mirrors. Jordan and Ethan pass from room to dimmer room, twist themselves into corridors, spiral stairs around their feet as crying girl calls them further into recesses and farther from the pure grace of waves that break upon their shores.

"This way," says Ethan. They climb.

Crying girl sits by a small window in the upper reaches of the house. Her hair lies matted with salt breeze; her cheeks streak with grief. She turns toward the door.

"Who?" asks Jordan. His eyebrows stretch higher.

She is daughter, she tells them, of God, who left her alone to watch worlds sail into horizons, who told her to weep for creation and wait until the tide of man turned. She is here, she says, to gather tears from all hearts and enable worlds to stem their sorrow. She is their concealed container, their diversion, that humanity may not confront their deepest anguish alone.

"Where my Papa go?" Ethan asks.

"In good hands."

Ethan drops his face from his face and shows the boy inside the house inside the mirror. A seed of manhood spouts there, but it is many years from a tree, and many journeys into a jungle of acceptance.

"He is your father now," says the girl. She points to Jordan.

Ethan turns. "Truth?" he asks.

"Truth," says Jordan. Crying girl nods.

Wind enters the window, swirls the girl into another corner of the house. Ethan and Jordan return to the kitchen. The sweet smell of pineapple lingers.

CONNECTIONS

Mr. Stone put his drink down. Someone had knocked on the door.

"Yes?" It was a girl, about nine years old.

"I like your house," she said. "May I come in?"

Mr. Stone nodded. She came in. He closed the door, went back to his study. The girl followed.

"Would you like a drink?" asked Mr. Stone. He pointed to the whiskey bottle on the table next to his chair.

"No."

"Sorry, I didn't mean...I thought for a moment you were..."

"Yes?"

"someone else."

Mr. Stone sat, picked up his glass, drank it, refilled. "What is..."

"my name?"

"Yes. What is your name?" asked Mr. Stone.

"Susana."

"And do you want to know..."

"your name?"

"Yes. My name," said Mr. Stone. He took another gulp.

"Not right now."

Mr. Stone waved his hand at the shelves in his study. "Do you like books?" he asked.

"Some of them."

"Would you like to hear a story?"

"A story?"

"Yes. A story. Would you like to hear a story?"

Susana sat on the ottoman and nodded. "Go ahead," she said.

"Once upon a time there was a man with a wife and a lovely daughter, about nine years old. They all liked to go shopping. The wife bought dresses. For the girl, they bought books. She had so many books that her father had to build shelves in her room.

"One day, when they were shopping, a man came into the mall with a gun. He shot the wife and the little girl. They died right away, but the father got away."

"How did he get away?" asked Susana.

"He hid in the dressing room with a new pair of boots."

"And the bad man?"

"The police came and killed him, I guess."

Mr. Stone finished his whiskey, set it down. A few houses over, a dog barked, then fell silent.

"I had a father," said Susana. "And he didn't come home."

"Where did he go?"

"He went to a gas station. A woman came in and wanted money. She didn't know how to use the gun very well. She killed the clerk and my father. He was wearing new boots."

"That's…"

"a sad story."

Mr. Stone poured another drink, gulped it. "And the woman?" he asked. "What happened to her?"

"They said she was a little girl once, about nine years old. She liked flowers. Her older brother was in a war and he didn't come back. It took a long time, but she turned herself crazy. They put her in a home."

Mr. Stone reached for the whiskey, withdrew his hand. "I had a brother once," he said. "He went to a war."

"There's too many of them," said Susana. "Wars, I mean. Not brothers."

"My brother came back," said Mr. Stone. "He opened a landscaping business. He went all over, digging gardens, and planting flowers.

"But one day, he said he couldn't do it any more. Too much happiness made him sad. He sold the business and got a job at a gas station. One day a woman came in. She wanted money."

"Can I sleep here?" asked Susana.

"Yes. I still have her room."

A moon entered the study window. Shadows from the trees in the yard touched the glass. A slight breeze made them dance.

OUR ACCURSED HUMAN EDUCATION

Discordant agony and calculated heartbreak. A scorching breeze, the ashen belch of god's last supper, blackcoughs past our makeshift bench on our boulevard of broken hope. Sirens crack the sky. The ground rumbles.

A shirt sleeve on my face. I wipe. And Lawrence, my father from another life, touches my shoulder. A snake came to my water trough on a hot, hot day, he says. And I in pajamas for the heat, to drink there.

Our fallen heavens. My hand sweeps an arc, brushes expired angels of our lives. You talk of snakes, Lawrence? Look around our city. Look...

No. Nothing more. A mute sickness smothers me. My language has forsaken my tongue.

There's more to life than destruction, says Lawrence.

His words tip our heritage clattering from its casket, but I hold no mood for more bones, and hardshove its memory into the donkey stands. And although he's right, it's grueling to see. My eyes have suffered heavy blows since revenge boiled over the border.

My thoughts. Lawrence knows them. Misery is a state of mind, he says, and I admit that I'd like to unscramble an equation for happiness, but my belief is bloodpierced with nails. Here, among the iron bones and concrete bodies that surrendered to shellings, all the broken teeth of humanity litter our senses.

Take a beat, a breath.

Another.

Exhale. The air still rages.

Wrapped in stains, a young girl struggles near and asks for a piece of bread.

Dry, spitless. No spare love.

I'm no Jesus, I say. I got nothing. But Lawrence stands, takes off his imaginary hat, bows as if a theater curtain were about to fall, and says a yellow leaf from the darkness hops before me.

How? I ask Lawrence.

How what?

Do you endure? Young girls only understand a mouth that opens its hunger for a larger measure. They haven't lived.

And they haven't died, says Lawrence.

That's right, I say. Some haven't. And they haven't climbed a barbican where the rooms stink of defenestration. They haven't thrown themselves from the height of their desperation.

And now.

Now I wonder why not.

Pause, a rare instant of quiet. One more breath. Another moment of existence.

Fall back in time. A spirit sneezes. I kneel before our bench. Lawrence towers above me. It's like a church, these streets, but without salvation. Like a god, this city, but without a reason to live. Wake to the world and pray for extinction.

Lawrence clears his throat. Get up, he says. That won't help.

He's right of course. Again. But before I can stretch my limbs, a bird lands on my shoulder and dies.

Now look what you've done, says Lawrence. A hundred years ago we paid for war with honest blood. Golden and venomous. My snake came from a fissure in the earthwall in the gloom.

My feet push me to stand. An unknown tongue runs over my lips. My snake, I say, is my sickening at what the world has become. He must be killed.

Your snake sickness or the world? says Lawrence. His face wears a skinred cloth.

Maybe both.

Maybe neither.

What do you mean? I ask.

Once as poets we proved divine, says Lawrence. But time ran a whetstone over our empathy and we slid back to the earth. We forgot our being. We lifted the skirts of our mindfulness and found a colony of indecency under our feet. It snaked, uncoiled, stooped, and drank a little more of our delight. If we had been strong, we would have beheaded the illness before it spread a crescendo. We would have told our fears that today is not the day, that tomorrow never comes. We would have dug into our traditions and extracted the beautiful shards of our past. We would have held them high. If indeed our city were to reflect the light again, we would have illuminated the candles of kindness. We would have insisted that our enlightenment be forever ignited.

Who's the pessimist now? I ask, and a foreign enforcer steps from a nearby walkway holstering his sidearm. You're not exempt, he says and marches off without another glance and fades out around a corner.

Let's go, says Lawrence.

Walk. The streets.

Streets once treasured, now littered. With trash and rubble. Burnt broken statues of children.

Those aren't statues, says Lawrence.

Damn him. My throat strains to strangle my sorrow.

Your blindness betrays you.

My blindness protects me, I say.

Lawrence shrugs. Dust rises from his shoulders. How glad I was he had come like a guest in quiet to drink at my water trough, he says.

Your snake again? I ask.

Yes. He taught me patience and compassion. He sought my hospitality from out the dark door of the secret earth.

It's not enough, I say. We've got to eat.

Lawrence nods. Over by the border wall, great bells toll the hour of our submission and great clouds of gray distress erupt with the bludgeoning of bombs.

And turn on the lights, says Lawrence.

They crushed it all down.

Of course.

Our teachings say we must despise, I say. My fist tightens.

And love.

Cowardice, as cattle do.

I confess I liked him, says Lawrence.

That damn snake again.

Lawrence looks around like an unseeing god. Don't judge me, he says.

I don't. I cannot.

But neither can I save my faith. My mercy.

A stone doorway, a snake's dreadful hole. I hide my head on the boulevard. Above like vultures extermination screams.

How worthless we've become with our accursed human education.

How vulgar.

GOOD NIGHT RUDY FOR RED

I don't take red for an answer. Never liked the idea. A car is just another challenge you must face when you cross the street, like the possibility of a storm if you venture out on a boat. This car, even though it moves like a bullet, doesn't have my name

on it like a chart at the foot of the bed would if I were in a hospital asking: *where am I?* But that *is* my question and the nurse – I haven't lost touch so much as to be unable to identify a nurse – won't say anything but *Good Morning* and *This won't*

hurt much. Never liked hospitals either. They dropped one on me when I was a baby. It crushed my foot and thrust me stumbling into the corridors which I can still see from the corner

of my eye. I can't turn my head. I think something broke and I'm strapped into the bed so tightly that my world has been rendered much smaller than I remember. They say your mind is the last to go, but that may not take

into account a car that moves faster than legs. Maybe I'm busted up inside, full of shattered vases. I remember 7th Avenue and a race against time to get to a meeting where I think we were to talk about my future with the company

I keep, but there's no such thing anymore. It seems I've ventured beyond my expiration date. No career, no family, no memory of much. A street and a car and a guy on the other side who screamed *watch*

out you reckless man before he vanished from my recall. Maybe this place isn't a hospital. Maybe this is the waiting room where I keep still until my life comes back. Maybe it's the backroom of a store where they keep people who haven't quite

died yet. Look. I could always run between the bumpers with a dodge and a graceful leap over a slippery spot to get to my final destination which always showed me another destination in an endless series of leaps and destinations, as if there wasn't much point in moving at all, as if one life were no different from another, just meat and steel on an inevitable course to collide. Not everybody sees

things that way. The nurse – I'm starting to wonder if that's what she is – found more words, at least enough extras to say *the doctor has gone home* and I foolishly reacted by lifting my leg and yet it wasn't there. It seems to have wandered

west where legs go to be by themselves just long enough to come to their senses and return, but in my case, I think it's not coming back. I remember a bone saw with many teeth and a sad but determined look on a surgeon, yet it might have been a dream. I do that sometimes when I'm late for a meeting. I dream about how it will all go my way and I'll get to keep

my job. It always seems worth it, to flirt with windshields for they are of glass and I am of meat and if you've ever been in a supermarket you know that glass protects meat, gives it a buffer between safety and danger. Therefore, I must be okay. I doubt that the balloons in my room are hallucinations even though they say, in standard black letters that march across their globes like adventurers, *climb on me and ascend to the next level of recognition.* But there is so little that I do recognize. Even the walls don't appear to be made of plaster and nails, but shimmer like a translucent curtain of calm plastic that beckons you step over the threshold into the next roomful

of life. I could go there. It could be fun, but it seems I'm late and must run across the street to find my future. The future doesn't wait for you. If it were a clock, it would keep ticking. If it were a car, it would run you down. Unless I could climb through the ceiling and ask the sky which way home. That might work. That might get my neck

on straight and my leg attached. That might answer all the questions I've had in my pocket since I was a kid. This could be my chance to be a genius among all the geniuses that passed before me and with our collective wisdom call back to the world to be careful of assigning importance to hurried meetings, and beware the arrogance of assuming that tomorrow will be another day.

THE UPPER COLONY

One hand higher than the other. One foot above the last. The ladder on the cliff goes on and on. The cliff rises and rises, the impenetrable granite face of a hardhearted god. If Alex or Valdo dared to look down, they would see a distant terrain, hazy and indistinct, long faded from their focus. They had started in the morning; it is now late afternoon. Thousands upon thousands of rungs, hours and hours with no ledge to rest, no crack in the cliff to even push their hope into. They can hook an armpit around a rung and heave air for a minute, but cautiously. To relax is to fall. To give in to the pains and cramps in their shoulders and thighs is to plunge through the pillows of scattered clouds below and watch as the land waits with the open arms of its graveyards to receive them.

The ladder is wide enough for two, and Valdo pulls alongside with a loud grunt. They each nestle the crook of their elbow over a rung and with their other arm grasp the wrist to keep the hooked arm from involuntarily surrendering to the pain that whispers: *so easy to let me go, just let me go.* They blow hot gasps across the inches that separate them.

Are we dead? asks Valdo, and the coarseness caused by his rasping gives the question not a plaintive tenor but one of hope.

Alex manages to shake his head. *I don't think so*, he says. The sky is still blue and the pain too acute. The sun steps down a notch. They wait with hammers in their hearts until they uncover the courage to continue.

***

An hour later, Alex pauses. *How much farther?* he asks.

Valdo climbs three more rungs. *I don't know*, he says.

And if doesn't reach the top?

We fly a long while.

***

That morning, in the pre dawn light, Alex and Valdo had passed through a thicket of underbrush. Branches and leaves scraped their coarse shirt sleeves and at times they had to fight the scrub with both hands. Some parts damp with dew, and sharp with thorns, but they pushed and broke though. They came to the bottom of the ladder. Its thick steel knurled rungs reflected the distant dappled light of the morning mountain. Alex had touched the ladder, felt a heat, and for a moment looked back through the thicket toward the world of everyday desires they had left behind.

***

Alex pulls himself up another rung. *What do we do?* he asks. *It's getting dark. We must rest.*

Valdo coughs and spits. *Look*, he says. *A piece of me starts its very own journey to the sea.*

Alex carefully takes his shirt off and with Valdo's help, uses it to tie his wrists around a rung. The denim is sturdy and they use their teeth to make a tight knot.

Once Alex is attached, he helps Valdo do the same. They wedge their feet between rung and rock, and hang graceless from the ladder, pretend they can rest. They pretend that they have not challenged a force that is much larger than them.

Long before the original gods came down from their cliffs to throw their blessings upon mankind, the lower colonies were born. They grew from belief that one plot of dry grass was superior to another. They assigned importance to their own desires, and disagreed with their neighbors to the point of disparagement. If they saw a route that may have ascended to the original gods, they either scoffed, or introduced legislation.

Alex quivers his eyes open. *Who said that?* he asks.

***

An ashen moon rises on the cliff and exposes two corpses not yet lifeless. The sky above broadcasts black with the space between stars and below throbs with emptiness. Below never existed and never again will be. The world below is a long vanished dream. Alex groans. *I can't go on*, he says.

Valdo scrapes his throat. *We've come so far*, he says.

***

Morning, with air as thin gruel. Alex and Valdo. All their breathing resides in the house of wheezes and gasps. The repetition of rungs and the monotony of movement puncture the universe, cause it to deflate into the small space between hands and feet. The universe offers no expansiveness, no infinite wonder, no astonishment beyond the ability to ascend another step of the ladder.

Alex and Valdo think sheer willpower can conquer gravity, can transcend their own limitations, and that they can live beyond the means of their dreams. But their dreams will shatter them into a million pieces of doubt and leave them unable to grasp the next rung of their longing as they toil on and on, the entire new day, thousands upon thousands of more steps. More pull, more ache, hour after hour, tread for tread, a plodding that has no purpose, no end, no relief. One sweating heartbeat after the other, one labored footstep over another's tomb, one ill-calculated plan to upset the calculus of the universe and send it spinning into its own void as if it were they and they were it.

They should have known that a stairway into the sky is infinite and there is no reaching the gods. The gods are busy baking bread or lying down to nap. That Valdo and Alex believe they may conquer that which has broken better men, holier men, stronger men, wiser man, only showcases their immutable conceit, their vast ego that speaks to them of truth in fictions.

***

But they arrive. At the end of the second day, Alex grasps the final curvature of the ladder and pulls himself up. He collapses like a man long trapped underwater. Volcanic breath erupts from his throat, rasps hard and rapid across his tongue. His muscles are slaughtered beasts. Valdo lies like dead sucking sky.

A family takes them in. Alex is purple and black from bruises; Valdo rants feverishly for hours. For three days the family feeds them soup, later vegetables and meat – and when Alex and Valdo regain some strength, they hobble out to see what they had climbed so long to find.

***

The Upper Colony sits upon a wavy land and runs off on one side to cultivated hills. In the distance, through buildings constructed of colorful tiles, with flowers exploding from every black iron balcony, the early evening setting sun casts its long shadows.

Music wanders between houses like a carefree tramp, encounters other melodies, mixes and becomes a harmony. Festivities and laughter spill onto the streets. Men and women walk in pairs or in small groups and discuss what appear to be serious subjects in a lighthearted way. The air carries a faint scent of lavender.

Valdo takes it in slack jawed, as if he cannot believe his trial is passed and the reward reaped. His face moves between transfixed desire and unmitigated joy.

Alex looks around, too. He sees a more reverent sky and a waterfall of reasons to bathe in the paradise of unbroken promises. In a plaza, a women plays an odd shaped flute. A man reads from a book to the crowd:

All were poets, entrusted with truth. When an illumination descended into their midst, they were obliged to spread its light into the shadows.

As he breathes in the miracle, Alex imagines that a more perfect moment could not exist. In fact, a more perfect moment would never again exist. There might be a thousand colonies in a thousand universes, each dedicated to the unending preservation of happiness, and none would reach the fevered perfect pitch of this exact instant in this exact place.

Alex turns to Valdo. *I thought paradise would be more tangled and wild*, he says.

Let's sit down, says Valdo. He points to a table outside a café.

Alex hesitates. *I ought to call my family*, he thinks, *let them know I'm okay. But...* he pauses... *I can't remember their names.*

Worse, as Alex walks with Valdo to the table and stares at the revelations around him, he wonders if it would have been more rewarding to lose his grip and plummet during the ascent. A thankless thought, but once you have wrapped your pain in perfection, there's nothing left to attain. The days spin without clocks and the years without spells of storms. All the agreeable flaws tumble back to the soiled earth.

Alex sits, counts angels in the passing faces. For now, he will wait, recover his strength. A few days, a week, maybe two and then he'll decide: if he wants to stay, descend rung by rung, or simply step from the edge and take flight.

KILL THE MAN OR KILL THE MESSENGER

Caleb lived in the shed. "Boys live in sheds," father always said, a scarred man with one good eye, "live in sheds until my god says when." Father was unschooled, rigorous, and committed to the shape of his faith.

Caleb was twelve years old. Sometimes on a cool night he stuffed leaves in his pants. Mornings, he cleaned his teeth with fingers in the creek after father unlocked the chains.

Father and Caleb lived far in the mountain, got by on traps, a few crops, and an occasional trip to town. Mom left for a grave years before.

"What'll it be today, son?" asked father. The tree shadows stretched west. "Do you want the book?" Father could follow the lines of letters slowly across the page.

"Yes sir," said Caleb. It was forbidden to say no. He massaged his wrists, helped blood flow past bruises into his fingers.

Father nodded, pulled the book from his coat, began to read.

Once was Abraham. Killed his son with a knife, a son born of woman and blood, returned to the same. With this price, Abraham entered the kingdom.

"Why?" asked Caleb, the same question he always asked.

"Son ran from Abraham. A sin," said father.

Caleb didn't understand why a father would kill a son. Sin or no sin, death ought to be for the old. Maybe son concealed a demon, a monster to be chained at night lest it hurry to infect with sickness a healthy home.

A twig snapped and a young woman stepped from the trees. She carried a knife. "Take this," she said to father who pulled back his hand. "A gift."

"Don't want it, who are you?" said father, a scowl dripping from his forehead into his eyes and onto his mouth.

The mountain took a breath in form of a breeze across the woman's face; her hair rippled. She didn't answer, turned her head, held out the knife to Caleb. "Take it," she said.

Caleb hesitated, took it, ran his thumb over the steel edge, used his fingers to caress the handle. It felt rough, like an old Cedar tree, and as strong. He imagined himself for a moment a king among vanquished foe, smell of bloody skin, last moans and testaments, animal panting, a summer sky, flies on their feasts, the sun just lowering, the intoxication of success.

"What do I do with it?" he asked.

The woman looked at father, at Caleb, placed two fingers near her throat.

"Kill the man," she said. "Or kill the messenger."

It was an old expression Caleb had heard many times. And father always favored the messenger. Outside thoughts, father said, were poison. But Caleb had doubts. His wrists ached; he often dreamed he was a bird.

"This is your chance," the woman said.

My chance, Caleb thought. "I'd like to go with you," he said.

"You can't leave me," said father. "We belong to Abraham."

"He can leave you," said the woman. "And he will. If not today, tomorrow. Or the next. A boy must leave his father sooner or later."

"I will find you, son."

"But I have the knife."

"You would kill your father?"

Caleb thought no, he would not; a father was both a pillar to hold a son aloft and a boulder to block his passage. But Caleb would walk and choose which. He longed to hear other voices, to reach others who lived on the shackled edge of freedom. Most of all, the brief vision of his kingdom lingered, and he wished for it to never fade.

The Recognizable Sky

They call it shrapnel in my head but it's a needle in my cerebral cortex that stitches my thoughts into patterns I recognize when the meat cleaver opens my heart and kills all the ghosts that hide out there, Doc.

And Doc says we'll figure it out together, but something outside my perception yammers to come in and I ratchet his words into another cubicle of my mind. Outside, a cloudless day stands erect and birds fill the air.

Wasn't always like this. Used to walk jungle on lookout for landmines with my sense of direction on full automatic and my ears on the enemy frequency of the day. Wasn't hanging from the rafters. Now days go bang and my bladder goes busted.

Forget it, says Doc.

Where were you? And a long answer filled with explosives drives itself into my skull where all the rap songs go to die because we ran out of tickets to an understanding.

It no longer seems real. Once upon a time – and Doc says you can't say that, but I say it anyway – the world flew across my eyes with its rainbows and beauty pageants but then another conflict made everybody cry for retribution and we sailed off to another perfect piece of war. But it was a bill of goods without a payday and we left body parts and goodness face down in a monsoon of muddy fields.

How's your new job? says Doc, and before I can twitch a finger an animal instinct leaps from my teeth and I make howling noises with my mouth and eyes and Doc jumps back in his chair for a second before he remembers, I suppose, that my cuffs are made of high grade steel.

It's okay, I mange to mutter, but my leftover sanity has bits of mold stuck to it and I may be in need of a new set of chromosomes soon. After all, every each of us needs a change now and then.

Did you take out the trash? asks Doc and the phone rings.

Yes, he says. Okay. Right away. And the twisted pair of yellow and green covered copper connection runs out the window where I see in the distance a corporal in fatigues with wire cutters poised to end the conversation.

Peace enters the room through the back door and sits next to me. I remember a show on TV when I was a kid where everybody in town wore ugly faces to cover their beauty inside because they feared exposure. At the time, I could relate. At the time, I could see their pain emanating from their bodies and gradually fading into ditches that fed pipes that carried the waste of time and talent to the sea.

That's a lovely dream, says Doc.

Not a dream, Doc. A screenplay that started false and became true. A tale of retaliation that grew into obsession. A story of young men made mad through the sheer exercise of will. Everybody loved it.

By everybody you mean?

All the closet boys and all the senators that buggered them. All the bankers who sat on thrones made of stocks and bonds. All the teachers who taught that resistance is a recipe for disaster. All the historians who said it can't happen here, again.

What else did you want?

To stand up and read the dial on the thermostat.

You killed them, says Doc. It wasn't a question.

Of course. The only cure for an illogical response is another illogical response. Full mag. Otherwise we spend an entire lifetime wondering where we went wrong. Why did we take that left turn in front of the train?

And that's what it's all come down to. A series of days.

There was more.

Indeed. A lot of us thought we'd come back whole but that was the optimism of few years and hard dicks. We all read the same books.

A door opened. And another and another. Then they closed as twenty years became thirty and forty turned its back on the suicides to declare them acceptable because sometimes you need to take the easy way out.

You'll never know the difference if you weren't there. And with that Doc shuts his mouth and stares through the window as a fleet of canvas trucks pass. When the last one rumbles onto the parade grounds, he bites his lip and offers an apology for his sterile clipboard and his incessant pen. But a job is a job.

Yes, a job. We all have one and mine now is to find out where I left a piece of myself. It's out there somewhere and maybe I can stitch it back on with the needle in my cerebral cortex that sutures my thoughts into patterns. After all, I still recognize the sky.

DOGS OF ANOTHER JAZZ

This time around Tuba had an actual bad feeling; he winced, as under his shirt, one of his wicked angels stroked the scar on his chest. Sure as a downbeat, the guys knew what that meant alright, but Tubs, for one, would have nothing to do with it. "Oh, blow me some bass notes!" he hollered with his big grin. "You can do it!" Tuba gave up a low chuckle. Yeah, he could blow them all right. Nobody better. He thumped those notes out of his horn like he was calling all angels in each of the seven heavens to join them in whatever New Orleans barroom they happened to find themselves in that week.

But today they were a long ways from any stage. They were way the hell out on some rural back road hollow – and once again they were looking for one of those god-damn deviant dogs. Of course they had to come out here to find them, but Tuba didn't like it so far from the city. The settlements were scattered black pebbles, the land was too quiet and still.

As usual, Piano was driving. It was his old blue van and he was the one with the connections for the stuff they came out here to collect. Friends and brothers though they were, Tuba wasn't even sure what the shit was. Some sort of mojo thing, according to Piano. Get you plugged in, make you a god-damn legend. Well, Tuba wanted to catch a break too, but sometimes he wondered if this was the way to do it. Mostly he had simple ambitions – his friends, good food, good music – and just thanked his stars that the Lord saw fit to kiss Tuba on the brass.

And Tuba doubted, he sort of doubted that Piano told the big shots who traded favors and gigs for this stuff where it came from – or how on God's little green earth-apple three jazz musicians got hold of it. In fact, he bet Piano gave it some fancy pharmaceutical name and let it go at that. Who could blame him? Nobody would *want* to know.

Well, maybe Crazy Danny who used to follow them all over town begging for a chance to sit in with one of his crazy poems he scrawled out between crazy cups of coffee he always drank with his two crazy hands. But they were a straight up, old time trio. They didn't go for that poetry shit. And besides, Crazy Danny fell off a bridge over the interstate last year in a fit of drunken October and bounced right into a pine box.

***

Up ahead, a rusted carcass of pickup truck. Tuba nods. Piano pulls up behind it and turns off the van. For a moment an echo of tire gravel crunches up through the trees and joins the dull thunk of doors as they get out; the sounds hitch themselves to a lone crow and fly off. The three of them are left looking around, sniffing the lonesome air.

Maybe something in the soil, Tuba thinks, something that lets these cursed dogs grow way out here, lets them sprout somehow from the sacred earth. Maybe Devil drips his hot sweat in these parts when he passes through on his way to a lynching.

Tuba's seen it. Hell, they've all seen it. A dog laying on the ground like some huge freakish summer squash, his fat white tail planted in the earth. And to think these creatures were meant to rise from the hand of creation and run happy through the bayou on the heels of varmints, not stay anchored to the earth by what must be a tangle of foul roots. *Disturbing* doesn't quite cut it.

Tuba looks around. The dogs tend to blend in, but they're always long and fat, they breathe slow and old. They're always so damn old, with a dense mat of fur you almost-but-not-quite want to stroke, whispering: *that's a good boy now*. It's practically *inviting*. But the utter strangeness of a god-damn dog growing from the earth next to real flowers and trees was enough to bring an empty pain to your stomach.

And though they've all seen them, doesn't mean they're easy to find. They don't pop up just anywhere – and they sure as hell don't last. They come up out of the ground first just a little puppy face on the end of a thick tail but within a couple of hours, a full grown Louisiana hound and a hour or two after that, already old and nearly ready for dog heaven. So you got to know how to gauge the light coming through the trees just right and watch for the telltale slant of shadows on the road.

But Tuba has the knack. And though he gets the creepies every time he gets near one, maybe these creatures are just another breed of angel, with a purpose he can't see. Well, probably some godforsaken purpose, he'll admit that. How could it be otherwise? Certainly not like those glorious seraphs he witnesses when he paddles his horn through a raging river of rhythm, when he feels the hot breath of harmony on his lips.

No matter, he's picked a good spot again. Across the road from the pickup truck and up the low hill a few yards, a ripe dog was growing next to what looked like an old railway timber.

As Tuba approaches, he takes a muzzle and a large hypodermic syringe from his coat. Muzzle's a precaution, normally the dogs are docile. "Tubs, give me a hand," he says. Another precaution. Tubs puts his weight on the dog while Tuba slips on the muzzle. He flicks the side of the syringe once with his forefinger, looks back at Piano.

"Do it," says Piano – and Tuba pokes the dog in the side with the needle. Dog gives a sleepy little yelp and the syringe slowly fills with thick white fluid. Tuba looks like he ate too much cheese, but there's a lot of opportunity in this little cylinder. A lot of upscale bookings where the party mammals fork out more than a few chapped claps in between the beer drafts and the dance floor.

Used to be these three never went wild on a big dream. Always stayed on the straight and Baptist narrow like Mama said, never fiddled with witchy weird or stayed out past 4 in the morning drinking the darky hard. They'd been friends for twenty seven summers and up until the last few months, would have never been out here skulking around on this not-exactly-depraved-but-surely-at-least-grue-some mission to scrape some more ambition into their pockets.

Piano started it. Tickled a few notes into the ear of that scrawny woman with the black curio shop over by the river and pretty soon she was spilling her olden secrets into the sheets. Secrets maybe best left unsaid. But Piano no fool. He scratched her back until she sighed and then came straight to Tuba with the old woman's Cajun boogie because he know Tuba got the touch.

Tuba grew up around these parts and in some ways he still smelled of swamp. But he left for the city, long ago. It was either that or live the same old comatose dreams, like your boots were stuck in a bog, slowly sinking until the land took the last of you and your desperate pleas were silent.

And of course Tubs comes along because well... he always comes along. He's a good simple oversize soul, a giant of a drummer, and he never fails to carry the rhythm. Without Tubs, they might as well be Irish or something. And besides, they're best of friends, an *ensemble*, a god-damn *jazz trio* for Christ's sake – and they have to stay together.

At first, this scavenging – hell, this looting – wasn't so bad and they had to do *something* since the hurricane blew most of the joints and tourists clear up to

Kansas City. But now Tuba's having second thoughts. He wonders if he should still believe that all things and all actions are divine.

He pulls the needle out and holds the syringe up to the fading light. It's full of fluid and the dog exhales a sound of hollow bones. "That's it. Let's get the hell out of here," Tuba says. It'll be okay with him if they play nothing but happy sappy love songs for the next couple of weeks.

An old man climbs out of the pickup truck covered in dirt and rust like he was checking the floorboards for beetles. His eyes are glazed, two unfurnished rooms. "What you doing here?" he shouts. "My earth, my dogs. Look, you god-damn killed him!" But he isn't pointing quite right. The compass of his vision is bent east.

Piano pushes his tongue through his teeth. It sounds like stepping on a snail. "Look old man," he starts to say.

"Don't you old-man me. I knew Blind Bobby Johnson. Gave him my two god-damn eye balls and bought his god-damn looks and luck." He steps closer to Piano.

Normally Tuba would have loved what happened next. It had happened many times in their twenty seven years. But never on a rural back road hollow with a stormy screwball of an old man, a syringe of questionable – well, some might even say *unholy* – spoils from a dead or dying dog, and the sun sinking into a Mississippi of trees. Always in a saloon, a good-time backroom or an old-fashioned burlesque show.

The band would start improvising, knocking holes in the charts, and get way out on a limb reaching for the highest piece of melodic fruit. Piano would run his fingers hard into his right-hand wall and start stroking the soundboard. He'd sharpen his notes while Tuba erupted deep Jesus juice into the air that then dropped like lava into the hair and ears of the mad stomping crowd. And just when they couldn't take it no more, when another few measures would have them falling from their high wire into a discordant pit, Tubs would come riding in on a kick drum tornado, gather everybody up in a whirlwind of tom rolls and cymbal stretchers, carry them safely back to the chart.

It was Tub's habit of rushing into a tight spot with his hands raging that started a chain of events that would leave them all wishing their dream of catching a break after so long had just climbed on the tour bus without them.

Tubs ran over, jumped on the old blind man and pummeled him with paradiddles against the side of the pickup truck. The old man started hollering something about snakes but Tubs threw him inside the truck. The seat was gone to a back porch somewhere and the old man made a watermelon sound when his head hit the transmission hump. Then a stunned moment of crystal silence.

"Shit. Let's get out of here," said Piano, backing up. His voice hammered a missing string. They scrambled into the van, and sped off. But in their excitement and panic, Piano didn't turn the van around on the narrow road and instead of heading back up toward the city where they might have had a chance to wrap their nerves in a bit of bravado, they wove deeper into the black back bayou. Tuba couldn't find his lungs for a while but his eyes worked fine and he could see how the last red rays of the sun painted the bouncing road with an altogether dark and diabolic brush.

***

Usually, Tuba didn't actually *see* angels, just heard them whisper or felt them scratch the scar on his chest. Like now. Even so, he knew what they looked like because once in a while they crawled out from under a church pew and winked at him. Tuba grew up in these general parts back when old Jack McCarthy still walked the river in his big boots, before he grabbed a cancer by the throat and wrestled it to the death. Nobody ever forgets that sort of thing and Tuba had learned to regard the angels as friends, even the ones he didn't want to be around. There was power in their breath.

When he was a running boy, one day Tuba tripped on a tree root and met the hard blade of a sharp rock right where his heart kept tabs on the front room of his breastbone. Damn near killed him. Maybe he would have died, but one of the spirits he knew from the woods happened by. She put her hand on the blood until it was no more than a sticky coat of harmless barn paint and even that she licked off with her giant black tongue. Nobody ever forgets that sort of thing either – and all the while she was spooky-tooth smiling.

Some say Piano once made a deal with one of the bad gods to get his own break from the business and go to Nashville. If so, he knew what the Juju boys looked like too. But Tuba didn't place bets on those whispers. All you had to do was use the eyes God had hammered into your head and see that Piano was still here. Still humping the elephant tusks.

***

They came to a large house and by now none of them knew where the hell they were. Nothing but dark, dirt roads, no signs. And Tuba knew, if you ask someone for a direction out here, they likely to say something like: *go that way until you get to the place where lightning hit old Hank on the head back in 68.*

The house had lights on, seemed normal. Why not? Just regular folks out here, right? Nobody's minding *our* business, don't even know we're here. Tuba tried to keep his idling thoughts from escaping with the van exhaust. But it was Tubs who broke the silence.

"I'm hungry," he said.

Tubs was a big guy, needed a lot of bread to juggle his sticks. Nothing new there. But it was the familiarity of the sentiment that brought their mood back from the brink. The words pushed aside a certain curtain and suddenly any gnawing doubts about the house scampered into the dark grass. Yes, it had been a long day and they were all hungry. And on second thought, the place looked *friendly*, nothing but sweet southern hospitality for sure, bet two biscuits on it.

And true enough, just as they pulled in off the road and got out of the van, an old woman opened the front door and motioned the jazzmen up the wide wooden steps. "Come on," she said, almost too easy. "Supper's about ready."

Outside of sculpting everyday air into heavenly notes that rolled over table tops into the lap of a pretty girl and made her smile, there was nothing Tuba liked better than a boiled potato. In fact, one night he had nearly got into a fight with Prince Parker at the Famine Club when the cook came out and announced that there was only one potato left in the whole damn city but that he had wheedled and begged and finally, to please his best customer, traded two chickens for it.

Prince Parker no lightweight but Tuba jumped up, grabbed him by his saxophone string and told him in no uncertain terms who *indeed* was the best customer in this place. Potato's mine, he said – and Prince Parker was so startled he raised his arm stiff and sinister before he remembered his legendary impeccable manners and patted Tuba on the shoulder.

"Of course friend," he had said. "You must eat."

***

The old woman keeps going to the window. Her chair makes a quiet dusty noise on the rug when she pushes it back from the table – and as she moves slowly to the glass, she pinches her face, seems worried about something. Tuba glances around.

Tubs and Piano have washed their plates with spit. Boiled potatoes or no, they might have picked the wrong house. Woman hasn't said a word. Best to make our polites as soon as we can, Tuba thinks.

But before he could clear his throat, footsteps scraped the porch boards, and the unease that had been building up in the woman's face drained out. Her features refilled quickly with relief starting with her lower lip and working up to her eyes. The old man from the pickup truck stood in the dining room doorway holding a dark rag. "Hello mama," he said. "How's your heartbeat?"

"Fine, dear. We have company," she replied. But he just walked past the table into the kitchen with his fingers fluttering the air in front of him. "Oh, I can smell them," he said.

Tuba leaned over to whisper. Stay cool, he can't see us. But Piano looked like he had spiders on his face and scratched his lower jaw with two fingers.

The old man came back with a bottle of some kind of white sauce and set it on the table next to Tuba. He put a fist down and caught the edge of Tuba's plate with his front knuckles. The plate reared up like a spooked horse and threw some potato juice on the table cloth.

"I knew Blind Bobby Johnson," the old man said.

"Yes sir," Tuba stammered. "A good man. Everyone says so. I mean, I heard that everybody... Uh. He treated everyone nice, you know... like his own kin... I heard."

Tuba looked around. Maybe someone else knew this story better than him. But Tubs had lost his fanatical intensity, was just looking at his pants – and Piano was humming *When The Saints Come Marching In* under his breath. Old man just pointed the inkwells in his eyes in Tuba's general direction and widened his nostrils.

If there was ever a time in his life that he needed one of his good angels, the kind he *wanted* to see, to come riding in on some sort of chariot and pull him the hell out of the pickle jar he had squeezed himself into, Tuba felt that time was right now. And if that god-damn good angel had a heavy thread, why she could just sew Tuba's fool mouth up bloody red and maybe the old man couldn't recognize his voice.

But Tuba knew they were on their own. He could tell from the way his scar refused to itch. And if he had ever thought that a little greedy ambition was okay and a little witchy-dabble wouldn't hurt nothing as long as you swore not to do it on Sunday, he sure as hell didn't think so now.

"Know what this stuff is, son?" the old man asked. Tuba looked at the bottle, shook his head.

"He shook his head, dear," the woman said.

Actually, Tuba had a pretty good idea what the stuff in the bottle was, or at least where it came from. Ever since he was a boy he had heard about Bobby Johnson, but those were just *stories*. Things a mama said to get you to shut up when she was tired. Tuba hadn't thought about that shit for years.

Blind Bobby had a place up on higher ground where he kept bobcats and stray dogs in cages. Did things to them. Nobody seemed to know exactly what, but they all agreed it was something spooky – with doctor knives. Later, he'd put the big cats and dogs together – and if the wind was coming out of Spanish Lake at night, you could hear their cross-breeding screams cutting through the air like two long trains derailing. They said if you tried to creep up there and watch them doing it, you'd go as blind as Bobby. And even though they were just stories, nobody had wanted to find out for sure.

"That's not quite right," said the old man, and Tuba banged his knee on the bottom of the table. "It was when they did it, when Blind Bobby wrapped his heart with their special skins, that he could see – you know, to find the crossroads again."

Tuba felt a tickle on his collar bone and reached up to touch it, to make sure it was sweat. Seemed like a good time to get some air.

Apparently Piano, who had recovered his calm and finished his rendition, agreed. "Uh, thanks," he said, and stood up. "Getting late, better let you go." He made a little breeze with his hand toward Tubs and Tuba. The woman started to open her mouth, but the old man somehow sensed it and patted the air with his fingers.

***

They open the door and drape three shadows on the front porch. Best to make quick down the steps into the short driveway. The night had turned a little stingier with starlight.

"You forgot your bottle!" the old man shouts and comes stumbling outside waving it over his head. "Taste it, god-damn it! It's good for you!"

Walking fast, they reach the van, climb in, slam the doors. Engine coughs and catches.

"I knew Blind Bobby Johnson you sons of bitches! He told me about you!" The old man falls to his knees in the driveway, tries to pull himself up by the sky. "He warned me you'd come looking for trouble!"

Piano hurls the van back into the road, his hands burning the wheel. Transmission sounds like a rock crusher. Old man gets one leg under himself, throws the bottle. It smashes on the wiper blades, drips white glop on the glass. He pulls a pack of matches from his shirt pocket and fumbles them until his hand catches fire. He runs up, slaps the window.

"Go! Go!" Tuba hollers. The van explodes into stallions, spins up snakes in the road, and throws a tire full of bayou dust into the old man's face. Tuba turns in the seat and sees the old man shrinking behind them, eye sockets catching the red glint of taillights, mouth spilling a furious mix of moonlight soup and spit. His clothes have grown too big. He looks like a man waiting his turn on a scaffold.

Piano gets the fishtails under control and stiffens his leg as hard as he can on the gas pedal. But something's wrong. They seem to be moving slower and slower. The engine thunders, roars, howls like a wild dog, but somehow everything just gets quieter and still. And as they look ahead to the narrowing road in the dark distance, illuminated by a few stars and two thin headlights, it seems they can see the end of this mad day getting closer. But they're looking through the wrong end of a telescope at what must be the whole incredible wide center of the universe. They can see how full of promise it is, but it looks so far away.

In that moment, one of Tuba's angels not only scratches but *gouges* his chest as if with a hot claw. Tuba cries out – both in excruciating pain and relief. The others sense it too; their faces change from blank fear to raptured stone. And in that silent instant, within that cacophony of silence, with a planet of trees flying past the windows, yet somehow motionless, a voice erupts into the air, the volcano of an overwrought heart. It weaves metallic echoes inside the van, and is seemingly of everywhere, the trio can't tell who or what speaks; Tuba, Tubs, Piano, the angel; they have become one, a quartet of shared desire. *With so much good love in our corner of creation,* the angel – or the world itself – declares, *and yet we risk everything we hold dear to try and catch such a damn fool impossible dream.*

AN ODD TIME MELODY FROM ABOVE

No time to beg her heart to jump from the balcony and make itself at ease in his breast pocket for he is near a deathdoor because time has filled him with six dozen birthday cakes and a case of colon cancer. He climbs up by the back stairs and grabs the girl by her dogscruff to make sure she knows who's boss but she pushes him into the balcony backwall and puts a hardpan knee in his crotch and says no rough stuff.

Wait, he says. I thought we agreed that rough was the codeword this week and that we needed to spice our relationship with salsa dances and trespass motions. But she says you are mistaken and I won't have it. And he says well okay if that's the way it is, I'll find another playmate.

But there are no more for him. He's old and goes to the bathroom too often and blames it on coffee not age but that's just for the outside world. Inside where it counts he knows the truth that romance is a once upon a time story, and now lives only in the heart, or as they say in the West Indies, the imagination. And she says now you're catching on.

What do we do then? he says. And she says let's take a class together and that sounds good so they enroll in How To Fix A Buick and before long they're both up to their old armpits in sweat and grease but feeling younger and more like rolling in the hay despite the smell.

This goes on for weeks and they're just about into the part about piston rods and camshafts when the teacher, a young man from the farthest reaches of Argentina, runs off with one of the students and elopes at the beach. Not even a postcard.

Looks like we're stuck with each other says the once romantic old guy. And the still romantic old girl says I guess so and they climb into the back of the disassembled Buick and make it happen right there on the upholstery.

Now what? he says. And she says we pay the fine. And he says what fine?

The one where we wake up in the morning with aches and pains for pretending to be teenagers again.

That is indeed what happens when you stretch your limbs akimbo in the back of a Buick at a certain age and even though they both knew that before they started they decided to take a chance for what's life without living? A good question and they both whisper amen.

Now then, she says. Let's think about living.

He nods. Let's think about loving.

Let's think about our own song and forget about the ibuprofen. She nods toward the jukebox the teacher from the farthest reaches of Argentina left behind in the shop and says do you have a coin? But he says I'm fresh out. My songs all creak and crackle.

No matter. They kiss one more time and a magic cloud erupts from the Buick exhaust and envelopes them in memories of another time that seems like this time right in front of them so they both jump up simultaneously, or as they say in New York, at the same time, and walk out of the now abandoned workshop into the sunlight where a thousand couples stroll hand in hand and arm in arm, even leg in leg, through the plaza of no regrets.

A hamburger stand sells burgers in the style of ancient Rome and they buy two of them with all the fixings, or as they say down in Louisiana, dressed. They sit in the plaza and ask each other questions with no answers such as do you love me? And how many times have you failed to reach your desire?

But they are happy and all gassed up even as impossible answers to impossible questions run away to find people with more sensible expectations. For the man and the woman have been in the lifeboat together for several decades and know the difference between infatuation and commitment.

Lets get a milkshake in Paris he says and she says do they have strawberry? They laugh because they are old and don't have the strength to swim the Atlantic. But they can enjoy each other here in this place and now in this time until the very last whisper has licked an ear and the very last piece of bread has mopped up the last of the hamburger sauce on the paper plate of life.

That sounds about right he says. Or maybe she says it because they are no longer sure who is the speaker and who the listener. For a lifetime they have gone in one ear and out the other, sometimes with a linger and at times with a rush. But there is power in the long haul and love in the short fuse that ignites when the moon sleepsteps out from behind a cloud to wish them a good evening, or as they say in the farthest reaches of Argentina, a good night.

And that would be the end of their adventure were it not for a miracle cure for prostrate cancer that snakes its way into the man's colon and makes him realize that despite all of their differences, they do indeed love and will continue to do so as long as one of them remembers to write a note on each anniversary that spells out in clear and compelling terms that life is not a plaything to be tossed into the trash when it gets dirty, but a hard celebration of truth that love may not conquer armies of revolutionaries come to take the ranch for the cause, but it does buy enough time to thank the lord for the new day that climbs the trellis and the hardships that grind the bones, both of which are worthy in their own ways of our gratitude and respect.

THE INVISIBLE CONNECTIONS OF SPACE AND TIME

Walking in the desert, he arrived at a rope. It was thick, woven of coarse fibers – and hung from the sky as if by an invisible hook. The air was clear, not a single cloud, and although he raised his head as if he were preparing his throat for the sacrifice, he could see nothing except the rope that shrank and disappeared into the heights of the sky. I wonder, he said to his hands, if it is possible to climb. But his hands didn't answer him. And the desert too stayed silent.

Hesitantly he touched what seemed a miracle and the rope changed its position a little, perhaps the width of an ant. It seemed to shimmer, as if it contained a single silver thread. He touched it again, this time with more confidence, with both hands, and circled it with his fingers. I think I'll give it a tug, he said to himself.

Despite her few years, the girl in the city knew that her brother was dying. The doctors had shaken their heads and backed out of the room. The world was not so old and one more death would not fill its ample cave of bones. Meanwhile, a drop of prayer fell into the barrel of prayers and you could hear the girl's voice in the splash. At the same time, a bell shook the air and the brother sat up in bed. I was a man, he said. A man with thirst in a desert land with endless sky, and salvation.

Through my fingers, I saw that the world is a wheel with many connected spokes – and someday I will grow to roll it.

THE CITY OF OPEN AIR ASYLUMS

Nothing existed before his blindness. The past too was sightless. For uncounted time he lay enclosed in darkness alone with disjointed thoughts in his dark world. A voice said wake and he stood, a boy in a lighted room next to his father in bed who slow exhaled a tubercular life. A voice said sleep and again his eyes filled with unyielding black. He breathed quiet and slow another long time in the dark. A voice said wake and the final fire in the world entered. Illuminated his cell. He sat alone, naked, adult. Skin translucent and spotted. Clothes lay nearby, he dressed. A stairwell, descent. A sign read Hospital St. Thomas. He pushed open the door to a city street filled with nimble light and life.

Can you help me? he asked a passerby and the person said no for haste of a promise to be someplace when a bell chimed the hour of agreement.

He walked. Saw great bridges. They rose in heightful beauty to grant ships entrance to canals that connected lakes that took their fill of rivers and gave the rest back to the sea.

An old woman sat on a church step and proclaimed in a loud voice that all the institutions had emptied and all the once wrong people were now right. She called for a moratorium on reality and promised to hang the sane from pier pilings that they may trouble her no more.

The man who had seen the final fire in the world approached the woman on the step and told her that he had recently arrived in citylight from darkness. He stumbled, he said. Perplexed. The metropolis enigmatic. Like something he should know but altered. She said have a seat and they sat together on the brickwork.

The woman said the mindful who walked with grace were torment and that they must be purged but the man disagreed for he had found blessing. Unsure of his bearings but blindness cured.

I don't know where I am, he said and she said yes you do. You're here with me on church steps that climb to altars where emptiness pleads for meaning that cannot exist.

No, he said. I was young and now I'm old. Once in darkness now in light. I don't know my name.

Go then, she said. To find your name and with it your true self. She waved her hand. Bother me no more.

The man who had seen the final fire in the world stood, said goodbye and walked further into the web of city streets that jumbled like colorful pens on the floor.

Five blocks, six blocks, seven. A sign read Names and he entered where inside a girl sat surrounded by books with titles like Revolution, Reunion, and Breakthrough. Try this on she said. John. But he said it doesn't fit it's too tight may I have one like Arthur? And the girl said yes and Arthur now named as the man who had seen the final fire said thank you and left.

Arthur felt a hunger and a man who wore a yellow coat offered him bread. They sized each other up, scrutinized. They sat on a bench in a triangled plaza with three trees and spoke of a holy ghost. The one of madness, said the man of yellow coat and Arthur the man who had seen the final fire said no. The holy ghost of reason.

Some things cannot be reconciled. You go here and I'll go there, said yellow coat. And with that their paths diverged.

Nearby an old man wore a hat and read a book with no name. He closed the pages on a finger to mark his spot and told Arthur that the city of open air asylums once had been a harbor of thought where poets and painters gathered in coffee cups and treeshadow to steer the vessel of humanity with their abundant observations of what rang true, what false, and the embellishments that disguised both. But came advances in poorness of perception as advances often march and those who took contemplation with their constitutionals slow drifted to other ports of call.

Where are they now? asked Arthur and the old man answered I am the last.

Outside a shop a man swung a stick and confessed he had unjailed his demons. Arthur asked if he might lend the man fire so his demons might therefore be burnt and beaten but the man professed his love. For what? asked Arthur. Demons. But why? They make me whole.

A woman sat on a bench and stared at the sun. Her eyes flat, steamrolled. Her mouth an open crypt. She spoke only with her fingers. Ten twisted silent orators. Daylight blurred them into staggering shadow puppets on the wall.

Oh lord, said Arthur. Surrounded by firelight and blindness. Encircled by madness, enveloped in judgments of what makes us give up our light. What causes man to renounce his faith. To plant dusk in the heart, entomb the mind. Gutter his senses.

He continued his exploration, his search among sidewalks and ragged ghosts. Indistinct remnants of his forgotten past pursued him. There must be reason here, said Arthur and a young man tugged his sleeve and said I heard what you said. You have branded our city senseless. What has happened here? asked Arthur. Freedom, said the young man. From what? Reality. Why? Each his own. Why? asked Arthur but the young man placed his hands over his eyes and ran away.

So few answers to many questions in the city of open air asylums. Only one book without a name. The devout worshiped lowgods, sold delusions, bought injections. Insanity blood dripped from cheap hotels onto bluetarp shelters and slow flowed congealed into shoes and sandals where it rose to lips that mumbled holycoded words to summon creatures that promised salvation.

It was no longer sufficient to place words in a sequence of solace for those who clawed the sky as if it were a ladder or those who spat on buses. A burden lay upon the world. Its weight created crevices and people tumbled. A tumor had ripened and swollen while Arthur had been blind. It consumed true existence.

Arthur the man who had seen the final fire in the world when he was blind climbed a high tower dedicated to the creation of deceit that created more deceit in a cycle unbroken. He stood on the roof and studied the sprawled city below. Ample beauty. Abundant potential. And yet lost. It lurched between real and unreal, between forgery and truth. Day and night had swapped faces.

Arthur lowered his head, cried for a loss. Unsure if his or theirs.

There it stood. A world of possibility, its opportunity freely surrendered. Its once locked doors to madness battered down. Maybe, Arthur thought, he was better blinded. Alone with his fragmented thoughts in the darkness. To make his own earth in the void. His own dark life of braille.

Maybe one day he could return and search again. All things must heal. Or if not, they must be destroyed by the final fire in the world. And from ash and red clay renewed. Recreated.

Arthur returned to the street and retraced his steps. St. Thomas. He climbed the stairwell, entered his cell, undressed. All inside was now without. And like a window that opens both ways all outside was now within. He could no longer say for certain which was which.

THE FALL GUY MUST DIE

In the seventh month we needed a name so we could pray his death to purge our world of pain and with his passing put the burden of our sorrow down. Our cancerous anger had swollen. He had detonated our goodness with makeshift explosives and left families to lift their valued bones from the rubble.

A name must be strong enough to loathe yet weak enough to overpower when the time is right. We would need to kill him one day. Some said we should name him Jeremiah or Joseph but that family tree toppled too close to home. Better a foreign shore.

A large book of deed and name written thousands of years before freed the decisionists of their duty to decide. They instead conducted a poll in the seventh month to ask the nation to choose from the book a name for the man we must hate and the nation answered Naboth. Easy to remember and a sound to drop simple from our lips.

In the eighth month we needed to fabricate a face to inspire our love of retribution. A face must be familiar enough to connect it to evil and distinct enough to avoid confusion and foul enough to provoke recognition into abhorrence. We needed a face to spread across the land. We placed dark eyes and determined mouth and leathery skin on a bearded man and announced that this is the face to hate. This face shall bone splinter our ideals into those we leave on the plate to pick our teeth and those we scrape into the sink.

In the ninth month Naboth emerged from the womb formed as we had wrought and he quick learned to spread chaos. Though we roared profane at his horror, we secret satisfied our sacred lust. For he gave us something to denounce. And declaim that there but for Naboth go our victories in life, and in the end his death shall set us free.

A name and face must creep clamber from cavern to cavern and when appear, appear only in silhouette to keep malevolence inscrutable and its threat murky lest too many submerged questions come up for air. The named face like a phantom must incite dread but like a peripheral apparition must be seen only sideways. To this we aspired.

In the tenth and eleventh months Naboth killed men and women and babies and goats. His bombs splattered innocence on maps. He proclaimed his acts revenge for crimes we had from heaven dropped on his children and we forged our replies in fiction and blood. A mirror is never wrong we said and what we saw for ourselves and what we saw for Naboth were perfect reflections of reality in a still summer pond. His expression blackened the sky. Ours did not.

In the second age, Naboth grew more devouring, his acts more audacious. Blood erupted from our ruptured tongues in our passionate rush to shout the words of hatred. We demanded our failings be cured with his death for he blighted every person with blameless flaws and we could not reach our potential. We could not cure ourselves until he was gone.

But as we struggled to keep our balance in a tilted world, our memory of distant terror began to slow fade. Our worries were closer to home. Naboth continued his campaign of carnage, yet like a fierce dog who cannot jump the junkyard fence, our fear of him dwindled.

A name must be strong enough loathe yet weak enough to overpower when the time is right. And for Naboth we had chosen wisely. And the time was right. We entered his house, took his now useless life, and fed the remains to the sea.

Newly reminded of his horror we danced and threw cocktails down our throats. The streets ignited in joy. Our lives would no longer be severed from success. But the wheel turned once or twice and in the seventh month we needed another name. And so we darkened our eyes with ash and searched our sacred book again. Just one more time. Then we would certain celebrate a final boot print on the endless path of our denial.

SLOW TRAIN

When the train stopped for the night the two men approached a boxcar. The taller one climbed in, looked around. Empty but for a few pallets. Okay, he said and the shorter man along with a woman and a child scrambled up. The child needed help, a lifting. The sun low tangled in the few desert scrub trees. Byzantium sky slow choked itself black.

They opened their knapsacks, removed hard bread and dry meat and ate. An occasional iron groan as the train slight shifted and settled. Darkness complete and thin blanketed they slept.

Get up, said the taller man. The train is moving.

It's not light yet, said the woman.

Doesn't matter. We need to get off.

They got off. A faint candle in the east melting the darkness. The train slow moved away from the light further into the desert west. They followed, walked booted and shoed and knapsacked toward the quickening day.

Midmorning they sat near an old stone waymark and sparse ate from their rations. Food remained scarce and they didn't know how far they must yet walk. Water they gathered from time to time from cisterns abandoned by the railroad. The brackish liquid from an infrequent rain or another age they on occasion held under a wooden cover sluggish seeped through crude mortar into a bottomless earth.

The train slow advanced ahead of them and when they finished their meal they took longer strides until they caught up again. Then cut their pace. The train tail like a diamondback rattled.

How much farther? said the child.

Soon, said the taller man and turned to look back. Only their most recent footfalls crowned with a frail raised cloud still visible in the desert dustpowder. He faced forward again. The train continued its deliberate march and in the aching distance jagged peaks climbed from the earthskin. Maybe in two days. Or three. Still a long ways off.

Night near. The train stopped and they climbed aboard. A different boxcar this time after the taller man had entered and found no evidence of what they did not understand.

Why can't we use the same car? said the woman.

I don't know, said the taller man. But you saw what happened.

They all did. A transient companion of no belief in the same car twice found missing in the morning, belongings intact and stayed, and they wouldn't take the chance after that. Every third night maybe. Nobody knew for sure. And nobody, not even the taller man, knew for sure what they would find beyond the far mountains. A refuge or nothing but more desert that led forever into the late afternoon horizon sun until at last they funneled into the hellish heat itself and perished like flamemoths. He only knew they must follow the train.

They ate, slept below the boxcar roof and its sublime hollow stars, and when the train jerked into motion in the dawnlight, quick climbed down. All but the shorter man. He stood in the boxcar doorway. I can't walk any more, he said.

You can't stay, said the taller man. You know what happens.

I can't walk any more.

You must.

I can't.

The taller man lowered his head. Goodbye then.

The train kept its cold iron pace and the taller man, the woman and the child watched as it slow pulled the shorter man further away, his head protruding from the doorway smaller and smaller until he finally ducked back inside and they saw him no more.

When the train tail passed, they stretched, adjusted their knapsacks, and followed. The distant mountains shimmered as if they were not emergent zeniths of a graceful earth but rather a desperate mirage of an imagined oasis, besought and denied. The trainwheeled landscape groaned and gave no voice to their hope. It only widened the enduring sky.

In late afternoon the train curved slight southwest and exposed the trainhead far forward. A distant iron skull of a serpentine Moses leading his catechumen into another servitude. The man squinted and tried to estimate the number of cars between the tail where they walked and the head where they had never been but the distance was too great and his eyes too burnt from the descendent sun. The train lumbered on.

Dusklight stretched long the blurred shadows when the train stopped. The car where the shorter man had stayed now empty but for his knapsack. They took his provisions and the taller man, now the only man, found another car, climbed up, looked around, jumped down.

Not this one, he said.

What is it? said the woman. The man shook his head. We'll find another.

Where did he go? asked the child. The shorter man.

Gone, said the only man.

The child looked to the sky. Maybe we should go there too.

That night the only man dreamed he walked a canyon filled with snakeskin. It crackled desiccate and wrinkled beneath his boots and rose as he continued forward up to his thighs where he waded sluggish and tried to keep it from clinging to his own skin now exposed at the waist. The sinuous discards coiled and drifted to his throat where they threatened to enter his mouth and indurate what little he still carried inside of his yielding grace. The car couplings thudded dissonant as the train rekindled its pilgrimage and he awoke.

By late morning the child sick from exhaustion. The man and the woman took turns carrying it. In the afternoon they had to stop and rest several times. Each time, the train tail drew further away.

When they could they ran to keep up, the child in arms. Hard going. By afternoon the mountains were visibly closer and they saw on the far foothills the trainhead slight rise closer to the sky. The parabolic arcing spine of boxcar roofs in places dull glinted. As the train climbed, each car that reached the incline lent gravity strength and the train slowed. It slowed and iron groaned, grumbled. When it stopped for the night they were still behind but they reached the tail, now at rest on the opening incline of the foothills, and stumbled through starlight to find an available car for the nocturnal postponement of their exodus.

Morning and the train climbed, the man woman and child in slow footsteps behind. At times the child in arms. The slope steepened. The train heavy with burden crept on its ironrailed wheels. Each slow revolution of each slow wheel enumerable as an intractable and monotonous calculation to fathom the extent of eternity. Irrefutable proof that life forever orbits the same axle and cannot depart from the trajectory of its fate. They climbed, each hour an age. The train ground and grated and squealed.

Five days uphill labored. Water low. The trainhead growl at times decipherable in the leaden vibration of the tail. A vigorous serpent worn down by its toil. Yet also a resolute inculcator pulling penitents by their slow endless footsteps to an invisible deliverance. The man and the woman and the child. Each step of conquered incline a small victory that immediately vanished, replaced by another smaller. Slower. Each night the boxcar floor more sloped and the trainbrakes more strained. Little sleep in the boxbelly of an animal they couldn't name or understand. A stressed sound of dying mammals.

Morning. Man woman child. Their ascendant shadows preceded their steps and stretched toward the train tail as it slow mounted the grade. How much farther? said the child.

Soon, said the man. And this time he might have meant it. The trainwheel tempo had increased. Almost imperceptible but the requiem had become a canticle. As if the distant trainhead had taken a great gulp of relief from the summit yet concealed and allowed a small measure of otherside gravity to assist its labor.

The train still up pulled a long procession though, weighted with the undelivered freight of a thousand unrevealed promises. The sun slow fell from the sky behind the summit and presently the darkness grew and the train stopped, balanced like a body draped over a horse between its incomplete ascent from the old world and its hidden descent into a new one. The man chose a car and they slept.

In the darkness the man awoke, the train quiet. The child sat in the doorway and moved its head upslope right and downslope left as if weighing the gamble between future and past. Faint starlight reflected from the scattered mica along the trainbed and gave the child a beatific impression of celestial contentment the man hadn't seen before.

The man got up, sat with dangled legs in the doorway next to the child. What is it? he asked.

Where are we going?

Over there. The man inclined his head toward the summit.

What's over there?

I don't know.

Are we going to die?

No.

You wouldn't tell me if we were.

No. I suppose I wouldn't.

But you don't know.

There's a lot I don't know.

In the morning, the train came back to life and began to crawl the slope. The man woman child slow paced behind, once again in submission to their seemingly unappeasable iron god that led them to a distant reckoning. The day trudged across the sky to afternoon. Little by little the train picked up speed as the balance of its burden shifted to the other side, toward the future.

Just before last light they reached the summit. The sun hung reddish low over a sea in the distant west. The man and woman and child stood abreast, hands on foreheads. Fleshy visors against the glare. Below them the train submitted swift to the uncontainable strength of its downward rush. Its tail was soon small, diminished, inconsequential. A lastborn prince who will never inherit the throne.

Far below lay a wide coastal plain. It stretched south as far as they could see. In a few places rock towers outthrusted tall and watchful like ancient sentinels that had petrified with the passing of their becoming. A river flowed from headwaters hidden in upper canyons of the mountain range and rambled broad across the plain to a wide estuary.

This is it, said the woman. Her eyes grew damp.

Oh god, said the man. He took a step toward the descent.

No, said the woman. We sleep here tonight. The man turned, saw her eyes, nodded.

Night fell and they slept at the top of the world beneath a blanketing sky. A first moon rose from the darkness to lighten their faces. In the morning they gathered their provisions and the small fragments of their lives. With careful steps they began the long climb down to see what the train had at last delivered.

PLENITUDE

There he stood, Simon Favela outside in the rain, looking up to clouds with no expectation of bread. None at all. He had hunger but bread didn't fall when clouds rolled with rain. Bread only fell on clear days into arms and baskets of people who lived only on bread. Good bread and vital.

Most days bread did fall. Some people stocked up. Not Simon Favela. He always took what he needed and no more. Wasn't a hoarder. Neighbor Esmeralda Olivar hoarded, but wouldn't share on a dark day. Wouldn't share on any day, dark or blue. She was like that, a hoarder, but Simon Favela tried from his heart to convince. He enjoyed to share.

Hey Esmeralda, said Simon Favela outside her door in the rain, through the screen. Give me some bread? I have hunger.

No bread today, said Esmeralda Olivar.

I know, said Simon. It's rain outside. That's why I asked.

No bread for you today, said Esmeralda Olivar.

And that was that as far as Esmeralda Olivar was concerned. No sky, no bread, no worry. She had plenty of bread. Others could too if they would hoard or at least stock up. No time for the unprepared. No time for handouts.

Simon Favela walked and walked some more. Got wet in the rain, didn't mind. Rain was pure and gave him pureness. Rain was real and gave him reality. He knew too, with bread came responsibility, responsible bread, responsibility. Plenty for all without hoard. Repeat after me, he said. Upstretched his arms. Plenty.

Bread not eaten can be returned. Returned if not eaten, simple. Toss a loaf into a breeze, watch the breeze repeat the toss into the sky where bread then moved across the land and later fell over there, shared over there, in other towns with other people who also had hunger and lived on bread when it didn't rain.

On a patch of grass lay bread. Simon Favela bent down and touched a loaf. White or wheat or brown or black didn't matter. Yesterday bread, wet bread. But bread was bread and vital. Bread was real and pushed away hunger. Simon Favela ate what he needed to push the hunger and tossed the rest into the breeze. But rain was yet rain. Bread didn't fall from sky when rain. Bread didn't rise either.

Next day rain was gone. Sky blue, breeze blew, grass grew. Simon Favela walked again and thanked the sky. Thank you sky, said Simon. Bread will fall and everyone will eat, hoarders and loners and squirrels. Everyone will push their hunger away. Everyone will pass the day and all will thank the sky.

Not all thanked the sky, though. Not all. Simon Favela was friend of the sky but some people complained when it rained. No bread, no reserve, no friend to say here friend have a loaf. Simon had no friend to say here friend have a loaf when it rained but he didn't complain. One day without. Or maybe a fallen bread found somewhere. The sky provided.

A young man sat on a bench. Washed his face with bread, washed his arms with bread, his feet, and the back of his neck. What do you do? asked Simon Favela and the young man said I wash.

But why with bread? asked Simon.

Why not? It cleans the mud from yesterday rain. Rain is mud and mud is mud. Time to get clean.

And the bread?

What say? What about it? Look. The young man tossed the bread with mud into the breeze and the breeze repeated the toss into the sky.

Now mud bread will fall, said Simon Favela. Over there.

Over where?

Over there in other towns with other people who have hunger.

So? My arms and face are clean, said the young man. He stood, walked away.

Simon Favela sat on the bench and watched the young man walk away. A bread fell nearby and Simon Favela had hunger. But the loaf was soiled. Stained and smelled with motor oil. Like an old truck. He couldn't eat the bread and couldn't toss it into the breeze either.

A week passed.

Hey Esmeralda, said Simon Favela outside her door under blue sky, through the screen. How is your bread?

No bread today, said Esmeralda Olivar.

Not for me, I know, said Simon.

Not for me either, said Esmeralda Olivar. Bread is dirty and I have hunger.

At the next town meet, Simon Favela stood. Some use bread to wash themselves or their dog or their truck, he said. Now we have dirty bread.

Let's make an agreement, someone said.

They made a vote. They made a vote to make an agreement to stop dirty bread. The sky was friend and they all had hunger.

Not me, said Pastora Campa, a woman of medium build and wits who had a store. My work is to clean dirty bread.

That's a good idea, someone said. Opportunity.

They stood and sat. Paced and argued. Argued for hours with pleas for an agreement of clean bread and pleas for those who cleaned dirty bread. Opportunity.

Take care of the sky, said Simon Favela, said. Sky is our friend.

Sky rains, said others. And we need clean bread.

We have clean bread, said Simon. Bread is sky and sky is bread. We must care for the sky.

At last the agreement was agreed. Some grumbled, but no more dirty bread. Everyone went home and the next day it rained.

It rained and rained and Simon Favela walked in the rain. Rain was pure and gave him pureness. Rain was real and gave him reality and reality gave him a thought that another town, over there, with other people, may still put dirt on their bread.

Our bread is clean but maybe their bread not, said Simon Favela to sky and rain. Their bread may cross the sky and cross the sky above us here in our town where we live on vital bread and their bread may fall.

Simon Favela found a loaf in a tree. Yesterday bread from over there. It tasted wet, tasted of wet dirt. A woman who walked by under an umbrella told Simon mud.

Repeat, wet dirt is called mud and Simon Favela knew. Our work is not done, he said. He walked back home. Sky is our bread. Our work is not done.

INSIDE THE HALL OF SENATORS

Right there inside the hall of Senators full of meat and presented to the cameras that pick him up and shoot a verdict of his face out to the world sits Mr. Stuart Alexander to testify before the political dinosaurs that will soon hobble out and question his beliefs and practices in the hope that they may stay relevant within their shrinking constituencies and maintain on their juiceless features the captivating glow of a television spotlight. Young Mr. Stuart Alexander, accustomed to getting what he wants, doesn't fear the senatorial relics that teeter on the brink of extinction. The world belongs to the fresh.

Do you see us? asks Senator Erstwhile, chairman of the committee and grandfather to at least three dozen boys and girls who have unfortunately inherited his fryingpan face and his overactive eyebrows.

You are barely visible, says Stuart Alexander. On the edge of worthlessness and sooner gone better.

I was talking to the cameraman, says Senator Erstwhile. We still rule the world.

Beg to differ. The world belongs to the fresh.

Seismic is what would happen if average Joe Carpenter or Kathy Clerk took the seat with its microphone and waterglass and spoke as Mr. Stuart Alexander speaks before the hoary and overblown ego-centric ancients that belong in tar pits but they do not rebuke him for he is both right and rich. Their kneepans crack when they climb into bed at night to dream of how they were once fearsome. Their private parts are shriveled.

Excuse me Mr. Alexander, says Senator Elizabeth Browning from the great state of cows and cornfields, her face plowed and planted. We are in charge here. Our mirrors do not have glass.

What do you want Senator?

Respect. And maybe a bathroom break.

Look Senator, says Mr. Stuart Alexander, tech kingpin and all around rich bagman but youthy. I know why we're here. You want me to break up my business.

Senator Mike Hanson flicks his mic switch. May I have a turn? he asks.

Chair recognizes the gentleman from somewhere it'll come to me, says Erstwhile.

Thank you, says Senator Hanson. Now, Mr. Alexander. Let's be clear. We only want to discuss the possibility of breaking your business and sending its pieces into parabolic orbit. It is for the good of all involved.

Dinosaurs are bones and crushed, says Stuart Alexander.

Excuse me?

All of you guys, says Stuart. And gals. You're all long expired, and the sooner you realize it, step aside, let go your illusions, go home to your family, give the new boys and girls a chance, the sooner we can get on with the future. You're all stuck in the past thinking about how you got some that night after the high school prom and how you could run around the block without an ambulance. You're still pining for the days when a man could beat his wife and kids. I bet you still drive a Ford.

I move to censure the witness, says Senator Bronze Age.

The chair has not recognized you, Senator Age.

So what? says Senator Age. I've got a mic switch just like everybody else and I'll damn well speak if I want to. I'm an important man, been chewing on law for a long time, tough law like the tough jerky we make in my home state of good tough jerky. I won't stand for this insolence from a child.

Not a child, Senator, says Stuart.

Well, you act like one. Where's your respect?

Okay Senator, I'll tell you, says Mr. Stuart Alexander. I flushed your respect long ago. When my brother and I went to fight in a war you wanted to keep your interest rates favorable and my brother came home with a death flag on his face. And you sat there and said no money for used up soldiers, let them collapse if they can't pull their weight. And when your turn was on the war table long ago in another war your father started you jumped right up and hid in daddy's pocket all patriotic dressed up in his cash.

Back when actual beasty dinosaurs roamed the earth you were there old as dirt already and part of the tribe chewing up lower orders with your dagger teeth and your prehistoric appetites. Nothing but evercrave for your maws and you just let bygones be bygones when your friends crime and lay down heavy time on anybody who steals a bag of pretzels. There. I hope that answers your question.

Is that camera still on? asks Senator Erstwhile.

Cameraman nods, holds up a fist, sings some Peter Tosh.

Well then, says Erstwhile. I move we strike the witness from the record.

The video's already gone out, says Stuart.

It doesn't matter, dinosaurs know how to deny, says Senator Erstwhile, chairman of the committee, an ancient force that cannot be easily bested. And deflect. And eat our enemies too. We will stand by our version of steadiness and infallibility. Let nature decide.

Senator Erstwhile bangs the gavel and nature slides onto the screens of the nation so that it may decide, form its opinions based on other opinions and upon denial of the dinosaurs who are as Senator Erstwhile says quite good at it. And excellent at survival. At least until a meteor strikes the hall of senators and wipes out outdated habits that vegetable dinosaurs chew like leafy bits of grass. Or, for the more cancerous and carnivorous types like Senator Age from the great state of irrelevance, like hard jerky or last year's cruel meat.

LOVE AND THE LORE OF AILEENA

In the beginning, God erected the Earth and heavens. He blew comets from his nose, carved river beds with his knuckles, and filled the oceans with giant drops of his own cobalt sweat. The work went on for days but when he finished all these tasks and more, he put his feet up and poured a cup of tea. When he finished and set the cup down, he created the angels.

This is the way

it was done: God went to each shore in the fresh world he had unrolled, and watched the waves travel up and back down to the vast waters he had poured. He used his great vision to spot a single grain of sand on each stretch of beach of the world that was different from all the rest. He gathered these unique grains and with them, wove a colorful tapestry in his palms. He then commanded his body to grow tall. Slowly, with his feet firmly on the Earth, he grew larger and larger.

When the smallest wart on his smallest toe was the size of a crushing boulder, each foot a mountain, his head the size of Saturn and all the stars shone through his eyes, he released the sand. As it tumbled and swooped through the firmament, its grains transformed into ten thousand beautiful blazing creatures.

Of these creatures

the most beautiful and blazing of all was the angel Aileena. She became known by many names as her wonder spread. The Greeks called her Aphrodite, the Sumerians knew her as Inanna and in some small cults they carved the name Mereditha on each other's forehead with small sharp sticks.

Although many thought of her as a goddess, she was not. She was an angel who came to the Earth as an instrument of God's hand, to spread her wet warmth into the chilly places of men's hearts. A lucky man could wake up one morning to find glitter in his beard and know that he had been touched.

In his wisdom

God had chosen many different grains of sand: smooth, white, round, jagged, black, coarse, yellow, abrasive, hard, brown, and soft – as seed for the angels that now roamed from one side of Earth to the other end of heaven. Because their birth seed was so different, some angels had the temperament of fresh cream, others of spoiled milk.

One such spoiled angel

was Jarmacko who rose from the black swamp where he had fallen and opened his crocodile mouth. After the sludge had drained from his teeth, he went forth among the tribes spitting out the only sound he loved: the pronunciation of his own name.

Not all angels have wings. Yes, Aileena possessed a magnificent plumage that rose from her back and breasts in a graceful arc and carried her gliding into the rarified places between heaven and Earth – but Jarmacko had only one small bad-smelling stub protruding from his right armpit.

Since Jarmacko could not fly to the mountain that led to the white gates, he went web-footed through the flatlands blowing the same low note from his lips over and over, like a dead symphony.

But God had keen hearing

and a lot of time on his hands. He appeared before Jarmacko one day in the form of a black scorpion. "What do you want?" God asked. "I dislike bad trumpet sounds and have come to grant a single wish that you – my flawed creation – may learn to fly."

But Jarmacko did not want to fly; he wanted other angels to come closer to the ground so he could grab them and pull them into his mouth.

Therefore, he said to God: "Let me touch the angel Aileena just once. With both hands, I will shove her into a wall! That way, when her legs are tangled and twisted and she stumbles about on aluminum crutches, I will become important!, and she will be brought down from the heaven you have denied me."

God is not

an impassive statue who merely nods the world into place. God weeps too. And when he heard this request, a tremendous rain fell onto the Earth. It cascaded down every valley wall and gorge. It filled all of the largest rivers and streams to their throbbing and sobbing banks.

God replied. "I am a foolish God of my word and in my foolishness have offered my most foolish creation a wish that I am bound by my enormous integrity to grant. Will you not recant?"

But Jarmacko would not withdraw his wish. He raised his boot over the scorpion head of God. "Give me the wish you have promised," he said "or I will crush you like a bad cigar!"

Of course, if had tried this, Jarmacko would have found his leg burned off up to his crotch. And certainly God was not afraid of threats. But he did want his creatures to love him and he did promise to grant a single wish – and so it came to pass that when the waters receded and the oceans had stopped their trembling, the angel Aileena lay on the Earth, her legs wrapped in thick bindings, her wings turned to crutches.

Elsewhere

on the Earth, the quiet angel Daniel wandered from one desert to another searching for any grain of sand that had not sprouted into a heavenly creature when God had let go his giant hand. For this was Daniel's gift: to see into cracks of stone, to find small seeds in the overlooked places.

Sometimes Daniel opened his wings and flew to God to say hello (and maybe have a beer if God was drinking that year), but mostly he spent his days living among men.

Daniel did not always have wings. When he first slid from the middle finger of God, and fell through the cloud cover, he had landed with his head on a rock and for many years could not even speak. But he used these years to listen to the rhythms of the Earth more closely, and the sound of hoofs as deer went invisibly through the forest. He learned to detect both the true and false patterns of speech among the patriarchs.

But early habits are hard to break and Daniel was never voluble, especially when he went to God's tent and lay down on the mat. It was there he took the lid off the bucket of his ear and let God pour any measure of knowledge in.

Ten years

after Aileena was pulled from the skies, Daniel came upon her nursing her bruised breasts and untying the knots in her legs. The moment he saw her, he felt a javelin land squarely between his first and his second true ribs. It seemed to pierce the center of his heart as a great gush of forgotten affection flooded his chest. His eyes blurred for a moment as he sensed his lonely wandering days fall behind him.

At first Aileena did not trust Daniel. She had been betrayed by the smallness of Jarmacko and was uncertain if her beauty had stumbled over the same precipice as her legs. She brandished a small pink rose at him: "Would I not be the last on anybody's list?", she asked, then sighed. "I could have been a contender."

Daniel had seen that movie too and knew the right thing to do was stay silent and gently stoke her cheek and hair.

But Daniel

was saddened too, and wanted to find a way to help Aileena. She was just as strong, robust and beautiful as she had ever been, but she had suffered a blow. And even angels are mortal, although they measure their days not by the calendars of men but by the number of grains of sand upon the beach from which they were born.

So Daniel went to God one day and tapped him on the shoulder.

"God, why did you do this?", he asked.

"I fell into a trap of my own making", said God. "You may not know it but I answer to a higher power, too. Somewhere far above even me, perhaps one thousand layers removed from this place is the outer skin of the universe."

Daniel mulled this for a moment. "Is there nothing I can do?", he asked.

"I'll crunch some numbers", God said. "Come back next week".

A week

is much longer to those upon the Earth than God, and so Daniel kept on doing what he could for the world, for Aileena, and for his own troubled heart. He polished Aileena's crutches to a brilliant shine. He rubbed her back. He maintained a low cholesterol diet. And every day, he went to the quiet pond to see if God had yet signaled him with a pebble.

One day there were ripples, and Daniel hurried to the Jackalberry tree where God was hanging by his toenails from a branch.

"Hello Daniel", he said, and flipped himself around, landing on the ground. "Walk with me."

In the jungle, many monkeys chattered. Some threw feces at God but it did not stick.

"Do you know them?" God asked.

"Only as the distant cousins of man, who themselves can barely see me" Daniel replied. "To these noisy creatures, God is a slobbering wet mouth that licks their genitals and their ruby red anuses. It's the master moon that stokes the tiny furnace of their primitive hearts."

"Yes. They have a very long way to go and I must keep the balance among the angels, Daniel. So if you want Aileena to rise again..." God glanced up at a passing bird and then nodded at the monkeys. "...as counterweight, you must descend. You must join them, become primitive."

Daniel thought this over for a moment and then agreed to the exchange. He plucked a feather from his left wing and handed it to God.

"Hold this for me, God. If Darwin was right, I'll see you again in seventy million years. Otherwise, this is good-bye."

The moment

that Daniel disappeared into the trees, squawking and slapping his behind, God released Aileena from her bindings. He turned her crutches back into wings. She rushed to taste the lips of the sky.

Once again, the world was aroused by her beauty. Men dropped their hammers. Excited children pointed. Leg-sore travelers sent their eyes upward toward this extraordinary feature of creation. Even the world-weary, tired of their tongues, were inspired to recite the words a sage had long ago made immortal:

A man's reach should exceed his grasp, or what's a heaven for.

PUNISHMENT

Morning appointment, my punishment. I failed to obey some commandments, not quite theological, not exactly secular, let's say somewhere between revenge and redemption. Well, that's quite a range so to narrow it down... actually, it doesn't really matter. They do it because they're able.

That's how it goes when we're too busy with pop buzz and food on the table to put much attention on matters of society. After all, a sidetracked society is created by people who have an idea of intelligence and wait for that intelligence to give them an idea of how to help each other, but in waiting, fail to produce. And so, as nature hates a weedless field, up sprouts a regime of unforgiving mandates.

At any rate, I'm running late for my check-in so declamation and admonishment aside, the guy at the punishment center wears a smock and when he cuts off my hand, he tells me it's for a grievous error of character or judgment, but not quite a sin, and that I can still salute the flag when the president passes. Being young, I thought youth were supposed to make grievous errors in life, that's how we learn, but the guy in smock clearly grants my inexperience is no excuse and the idealism I wear on my sleeve a wholly defective garment.

Look, I know there are rules we must observe and others, to retain our humanity, violate nakedly, but I seem to be out of step with this fashion of obedience, and

I don't mean any disrespect, except that I do, but secretly and securely in my bed at night when I dream of freedom to write my own words on the wall or to adore an open expanse of love with those I find pleasant and welcome.

When he cuts off my other hand, he tells me that he exalts me so large that he can't bear to see me in the cold, outside his devotion, and that I can still push red buttons like colorful toys to launch a synthetic election. I can still hug a statue and caress black marble walls of bank buildings.

True, these are things I enjoy, but I prefer them on my own terms, my own rules of engagement, but that's a somewhat military phrase and I'm a pacifist, so let me simply say give me freedom, what we sometimes call liberty, like the statue we once thought grand or the bell we cracked with its clapper to summon the faithful. If not that, I would at least like to know my crime, perhaps be amused by it, and when I inquire politely of my offense, the one I must have stumbled over somewhere, the guy with the smock, his face full of duty, informs me that there are fingers we must amputate, and others, to retain our dignity, must wave and wag.

Well, that's no help, especially since he placed me in his calculation. I'm not we. I don't want to chastise my neighbors, or tell the young girl on the corner she can't bargain what she wants. I say live and let dance, let others pluck their own strings, march on city hall if they want, stay out past curfew, although, come to think of it, I do reprimand those who step on grasshoppers or kick their cat.

It's possible I don't see the advantage of compliance, conformity. Maybe there's reward at the end of the rule book. Stranger things have happened I suppose, though not to me, and the man in the smock, as if he knows my curious thought, exposes a heretofore unknown benefit when he cuts off my foot and mentions that now no boot shall be my master, no sandal my priest.

That's novel, I admit, and in admitting, realize my heart has been solely concerned with my own comfort, my own desires, and that I have at times failed to fall down, prostrate myself before the book of bile that men and women like the man in the smock tread upon and hold to their breasts to justify their cruelty, but I have just named them cruel, and in doing so, have exposed myself as a fraud of conciliation, and therefore have not yet abandoned my individuality.

It seems the man in the smock and I have come to an agreement of sorts, a disciplinary covenant, though not enforceable, at least not from my end of the bargain, between punisher and punished, that allows him for a moment to set down the tools of his trade and offer some discretionary advice of how, if one eye offends me, I can remove it myself voluntarily and still see the beauty of bullets that fondle red chests of nonbelievers.

Most I can do here is nod because I don't want to carve out an eye and plus, it doesn't offend me. I like what I see and, not to be discourteous to other senses, what I hear, although we know, my generation that is, that there are hymns we must chant, and others, to maintain our respect, must condemn as discordant and coarse.

Even though I only nod, suspicion must wrinkle my face because the man in the smock cuts off my ear, and as he slices, weeps, he says, for my obstinate skepticism, for my lack of faith in his faultless doctrine. Open your belief to our hammer, he says, to our blessing. Here are gods we must worship in harmony, and others to punish for crime. I am sad to see you maimed, in sight of rapture, and far from Jericho.

Certain, I don't care to see him sad, anyone sad I guess, even a righter of wrongs, but it could be a ploy to inhale his polluted goodness because I see no passage of tears, and I still remember my father who kissed the headlines of his day and returned with a dead purple face.

Now forgive the bad joke of my forearm stumps, but it's out of my hands now. I walked an uneven road for all my young years, cloaked, like all young souls, in my own protection, excused from decrees and directives. And now when the man in the smock cuts off my breath with a rope on my neck, he waits and waits as I drowse into airless slumber, a sentinel to my pain, my grief both holy and profane.

I'd like to stay and taste the wind, but now at least I know. When a punisher conceives the inconceivable and slinks away, he excretes his shame, names himself noble, and begs for a god, any god, to tally as virtue each drop of life that falls from his knife to make fruitful his love's barren tundra.

THE DEFIANT LIGHT

This new era makes me old, my brother Khalid says. I had a nimble sense of grace and now my chest feels boulder weight. It's as if the world collapsed on its side and we are lying down when we should be standing.

It's your pain, Khalid. A feast of tears. The world has moved on.

It has, he says. We face an angry act of providence that compels us, all of us, to feel our connected sorrow. Look around, Hamid. Look around.

On the bench where we sit in front of a barber shop on the avenue of giants the morning slanted sun fingers the dusty street. Feet joined through legs to drab faces pass. Once we steered our own roads, taught them which way to run. Bicycles made hopeful songs of spokes. These days compliance is the trumpet note we blow and dissent a cause for castigation.

Khalid taps my arm, gestures to the street. Every time I hear them speak, he says, my throat fills with birds. My stomach retches and everything I learned in school flies out. It's nothing but troubles they transmit.

Please. Don't forget your past, brother. It teaches us.

Yes, by contrast, that we live in an age of sickness.

A new disease, I say.

It's my sickness too, Hamid. My sickness of loss. It puts graves in my eyes.

She died as she lived, I say. And we still recite her many names.

A beggar approaches the bench, no words but those in the palm of his out-stretched hand. Go away, I say. We've no time. He turns and with one shoe missing, or one shoe found, retreats.

My daughter did nothing wrong, says Khalid.

She broke the law, I say.

Some law must crumble to broken bricks.

Of course he is right and I once agreed to express my agreement, to give it substance and weight, before they forced me to whisper anguish for my only son. They slashed his legs and issued threats that he may never grow to manhood if I stood in the way of their plan, harmony patrolled and purchased on the streets with bolder bullets. They offered my son in exchange for my surrender, my retreat. I could run through the rain for the last train out of my rebellious world and listen to the axles rumble as my beliefs crumbled to their own broken bricks. We will burn the sticks with which we beat slaves at the altar, they promised. It was love as dagger and worship as whip, but I agreed and saved my son while Khalid my brother let his daughter roam into the harsh arms of commandments.

It's everywhere, says Khalid. Look around, Hamid. Look around.

My brother is right and I know his loss is strength, and mine weakness. I wet my eyes with blindness for all the people on their knees, the present day in hand, that drives with its demands mad our throats and stomachs which, united, attempt to purge the bile we have sanctioned through silence.

My son is safe, I say.

Khalid stands, walks a pace, turns. And my daughter gone, he says. An old woman with a donkey passes.

At least you still have your wife, Khalid. I can't lose my son.

Of course, he says. He sits again, touches my cheek. Many losses, one heart.

If only it were that easy, I say.

It is, says Khalid. Throw out your faith and the conflict it preaches. Reject the lie that we must hurl our freedom against the killing wall.

In thirty years my son is me, I say.

All the more reason, Hamid.

With that simple truth, like a broken drum I have no sound. My tongue sleeps as dead on a bed of fear. I traded my truth for safety. I gained a son and lost a man. The sun now higher in the sky judges me. It splits me into two slabs of hesitation and asks in silent radiant speech if I will continue to hide in the compliant shadows or step once more into the uncertain and defiant light.

FINAL ARRIVAL

When I got off the plane in Astrakhan, the airport terminal was completely deserted. It was about 1:00 a.m. and I had expected few people but this degree of emptiness was a little unsettling. I followed the signs – they were in both Russian and English – down the corridor to the customs office. Nobody was at the counter. After I called out once or twice without success, a woman came in through the door I had entered, walked behind the counter, and approached me.

"Yes?" she asked.

"I just arrived," I said. "I'm here to get my paperwork processed." I laid my passport and travel documents on the counter, slid them over.

She rustled through the papers for a moment. "Where are you coming from, Mr. Bloom?" she asked.

"Germany."

"Yes, but what city?"

I paused, couldn't remember. My wife had arranged the tickets from Mexico. "I don't remember," I said.

"We must have the name of the city," the woman said.

"The plane just landed. It flew here directly. Can you look it up?"

"Yes. But I need you to tell me."

"I don't remember."

"Then think about it, Mr. Bloom," she said. "And when you are ready, you can let me know." She waved her hand toward the other side on the room. A line of gray plastic chairs were bolted to the floor there.

I walked over, sat down, tried to remember. It was late. I was tired. It seemed I had left our home in Tepotzotlán ages ago. I had passed though airports in the United States, London, and later Germany. It was mostly a blur. I had eaten in the German airport as I waited for my connection. The name of the city should be on my ticket, but for some reason, I couldn't find it. I flipped the ticket over, examined it front and back. The city wasn't listed there.

I went back to the counter. The woman was leafing through a booklet. I laid my paperwork down again. "Yes? she asked.

"Look," I said. "I'm tired. I've been traveling all day and I didn't pay much attention to my layover in Germany."

"I'm sorry, Mr. Bloom. I'm just following the rules."

"But I was the only passenger on the plane." I wasn't sure what that had to do with anything, and having said it, it suddenly seemed quite... unusual.

"Yes, Mr. Bloom," she said. "I know. That's why they called me in at this hour. To receive you. I could have been sleeping."

"Oh, I'm sorry for your inconvenience, Miss."

"That's okay," she said. "I get paid whether you pass through customs or you don't."

"How can I not?"

"Not pass?"

"Yes. Not pass. How can I not pass through customs?"

"By not remembering your city of origin."

"I was born in Los Angeles, California."

"The city where your flight originated, Mr. Bloom. Now, I've already explained. Please try to remember and when you are ready, let me know."

"But I can't," I said. And I truly could not. I remembered the German airport, walking through it, impressed by how it radiated efficiency and purpose. It was well lighted. The corridors were broad with shops on both sides. I ate a piece of chicken and washed it down with a Coke. I spoke to nobody except the cashier. Which seemed peculiar because I must have exchanged a few words with the gate attendant. I guess I must have been very tired then, too. I don't remember getting on the plane but surely I passed through the usual procedure. The ticket. The boarding pass. The *have a nice flight*. The seat. The seat belt. The acceleration pushback. The whine of jets. The dimmed lights once airborne. The occasional soft chimes.

I gathered my papers and returned to the plastic seats. I began to think using an old trick of mine. I started with the first letter of the alphabet and tried to think of any city in Germany that started with that letter. Nothing. On to the second letter. Bremen, Berlin. No, those didn't sound familiar. Bern. No, that was in Switzerland. Munich, Mannheim. Damn, I had jumped ahead.

I went back to the second letter to see if I had missed something, and then on to the third. My head hurt, but I'd figure it out. I'd done this many times. When I had the right name, it would enter my mind with a flash of recognition.

Yet I became distracted. Three other passengers had approached the woman at the counter. She was busy looking through three sets of papers and passports. I got up and walked over with the intention of eavesdropping. Maybe I would overhear something to help untangle my memory.

My plan failed. They spoke in Japanese, a language I could identify but couldn't understand. It seemed odd that the young Russian woman behind the counter could speak so many languages but I supposed in her position it was necessary. Her voice was calm and musical, like a quiet concerto. She stamped their passports and papers, and then with a gesture sent them to the far end of the customs area where they pushed open the door and passed through, presumably to the main terminal where one could walk outside and hail a cab. After she filed something in a drawer beneath the counter, she looked up.

"You are still here, Mr. Bloom," she said.

"I've been trying to think," I said. "I think it was somewhere north of Mannheim."

"The name, please."

"Maybe Frankfurt." But that didn't sound right.

"The name, please."

"I don't know. I didn't arrange this trip. I'm not even sure why I'm here. I wanted to get away for a while I think, but I'm tired right now and would like to sleep."

"There is no sleeping here," she said.

Although I *was* very tired and wanted to sleep, what I really wanted was my mind to snap out of its stupor.

"This is Astrakhan, isn't it?" I asked.

"Why do you ask, Mr. Bloom?"

"I've come to see the Trinity Cathedral."

"I'm sorry, Mr. Bloom," the woman said. "I am not a tour guide. Once you are outside, I'm sure you can find someone to assist you."

"But I can't get out," I said.

"I just need the name."

"I've told you. I don't remember."

"You must."

"Or what?" I asked. My voice rose a notch.

"If you cannot remember the name, you will wait here until you do," she said.

"What do you mean? How long?"

"Until you tell me the name."

That couldn't be right. "May I speak to your supervisor?" I asked.

"There is no one else." Her face had lost its friendliness.

***

Calm, I told myself. *Take a breath*. I went back to the chairs, sat, made a pillar of two fists, rested my head on it. This was a problem I could solve. Unless – and here I hesitated – that was only a creeping and wormy false confidence. I had already been through my mind step by step, piece by piece. I simply could not remember how I got here or even what had seized me to come to Russia.

Yet I must. A run for the door wouldn't work. I would certainly not get far. If I even made it into the main terminal, they would drag me back here where I would not be permitted to leave – or even to sleep apparently – until I could remember the last few hours of my life. I hoped it was a life worth remembering, but I was too exhausted to be sure.

If I could just close my eyes for a few minutes and drift to the place where lost thoughts are hidden. Watch flowers or birds while my mind kept churning. But that could take days, months, maybe years.

No. I couldn't wait here forever. I couldn't spend the rest of my days dredging for a minor detail as I passed from one place to another where now I'm not even sure I arrived.

My life waited. It waited for me. I needed to eat a carrot, chat with friends, watch a movie, plant a tree, have a child, smell the rain. I couldn't stay here.

But I was trapped by... what? A simple missing fact? What if it didn't even exist? *Please hurry*, I said to my mind. *Please hurry*. Patience was turning to impatience which was spinning into fear.

My mind needed time. I knew this. And entombed in this... place, I had plenty of time to give, maybe an inexhaustible supply. But that couldn't be true. No matter the size, the ocean of time each person sails upon eventually dries.

Yet as I sat on a hard plastic chair in a terminal that refused me passage, perplexed and spent, I began to think I was an exception to the mortal rule. My ocean was bottomless, my time unending. I *could* stay here forever, immortality purchased by paralysis.

And I wanted life without cease as much as anyone, but not under these condi-tions. The cost was too high. I may have been like a god with endless days in my future but if so, I was a feeble one, stuck in a gray room, waiting for a mundane detail to set me free. Waiting for the sun to move across the sky again and let me walk once more among the living world of April and apple blossoms.

SECRET WATCHERS OF OTHER LIVES

They say you can't turn back the clock, but Hector knew better. At night, as he moved from building to building, window to window, to observe unfolding secrets of ordinary people that hid behind their curtain cracks, he always encountered a peculiar sensation that started in his calves and moved into his upper chest. It reminded him freshly of life when he was a young boy which, outside of these excursions, he could never fully grasp.

These glimpses gave him goose bumps. They needled a dream closer to reality, a dream that people would one day stop hiding their true nature, expose themselves for who they really were, soft bellied up, like frogs on a science table. *It wasn't aberrant to dream*, Hector would whisper to himself from the shadows, *only deviant to pretend to be pure.*

They say a sharded vessel of humanity can never be repaired, but Hector sat fat-first on this timid platitude of rabbits and pronounced himself free. He had found an exit from the savage ruins of his childhood.

***

His friend Winton agreed.

"You're a god," said Winton. He sat next to Hector on the steps of the cathedral. The sun was out; the streets busy.

"Not a god Winton. Just three men inside one body filled with cheese dogs and a desire to see the world tip."

"Into righteousness?"

"No, honesty will do."

When Hector was five, his father had furiously whipped him with a belt for a season of ten minutes that lasted twenty years in his heart for a lie about who had let the dog into the house. This punishment drove Hector to the far edge of life.

"Want to see a movie?" asked Winton.

Hector blew scoff from his nose. "That's money we don't have and besides, real life is inside the houses at night."

"One day they're going to break you into a thousand pieces."

They might, thought Hector. An angry husband or an ardent cop. They might catch Hector outside a window with his teeth clenched or with tears of joy on his face. He'd seen it all, the outside observer of falseness and fact.

"Come with me," said Hector.

"No, I don't think so."

"Please Winton. You must. It's all we got left."

Winton reached for a nearby cigarette butt, almost a halfer, lit it, blew a little smoke, looked left and right before he nodded. These two, vagrants of an indifferent city, spent their days picking up discarded pieces of other lives and patrolling when they must for a temporary job. They found sense in uncommon places.

**

When the sun died for the day and subways drove workers from the cars onto platforms and the smog cooled and the dinner dishes scraped and the lights in the bathrooms turned off, Hector and Winton stood outside in the severing darkness. They watched through pale blinds as people undressed, read a book, put knives in their spouses, pretended their life was precious or at least wasn't wasted, and kneeled before a statue with their head bowed. They watched lone mothers rinse dread from their faces and contemplate the mirror that exposed tomorrow as another today.

They moved through the city and watched through the night. It was story after story, naked truth after truth, until midnight at last fell prey to the quickening before dawn.

"What do we do?" whispered Winton. He ached.

"Nothing," said Hector. "We can only watch."

It made no sense to Winton. "Why don't they do something?" he asked.

It made no real sense to Hector either, and he didn't have an answer to a question that had lurked in the backroom of his thoughts for most of his life. It had something to do with masks and illusions. "They probably ask the same thing of us," he said.

"Yeah, maybe all hope is dead."

"It's not, Winton. If they knew what we know, our shared scars, they might let the mask drop." It was an infant idea, possibly miscarried, Hector admitted. Maybe only a reckless craving.

***

They say that all the beautiful people once lived on the street and pulled themselves up solo into their singular beautiful existence, but Hector knew that was a myth for sure. It took the whole city and by extension the world to weave both the ugly and the divine. If we could put our hearts into our hands when we shake, Hector liked to say, maybe we could see ourselves, flawed creature to creature, no curtain between us.

As the sky began to smolder and illuminate the tops of towers, Hector and Winton walked to the bus station, lay down with broken benches and slept. The city was quiet for now. It was a moment of calm, a lull between one life and another. It was a pleasant moment of forgetfulness, but it wouldn't last. Soon day would take the city by the shoulders and shake, spilling people from their buoyant dreams into the light.

THE DESERT GARDENS

I came to these gardens to lay my darkness down, to brush my fingers through the wisdom of trees. I came to share my tongue with the strata of boulders and savor their fragrant histories.

I found here companions in caves and quicksand. I found them in shadows of ships – and crying the wet mouths of doorways.

When I am cast from this life into other embraces, find an honest man to carry home, or any child I have touched. Bring them to my bedside; they inherit my tomorrows without ending – and without ending, forgive my imperfect creations.

***

In another past, I met people living as ghosts in train yards of burning pallets and marveled that they still counted their blessings.

Here we are fortunate, an abundance to eat. We blanket our beds with love – and cherish our neighbors.

If you must, think only of those outside the gardens who live in fear of illumination – as if illumination might force a shuttered window of their vision and guide them from the poverty of their thoughts.

***

In hills of Appalachia I walked a long forest. Nightingales put their ballads to breezes and I wrapped my contentment in their choruses. I had hope mankind could retreat from its war.

So I came to know this stillness, this symphony of natural breathing. Days ran like rivers through me and my blood was cleansed.

My blood became a living thing of its own – and when I dipped my mouth in lakes, the water carried me to canyons, cradled me to seas where I crossed a thousand currents and swam the spawning beds of rivers into the thirst of strangers.

***

We are all the man with a family of adorable misfits who cuts my roses and calms his concerns when he plunges his scissors into the soil. His troubles are my troubles and in this we quiet our differences.

No saying how this will end. Life gives us a wheel and we spin it. With twenty nine summers in my eyes, life gave me an encounter and a chance to trust in angels. Like a knife that hurts and heals, I buried this trust inside my chest.

A few moments shall pass when I die to explain that angels have since possessed me.

It's something you can't take back.

They flooded my failings with light when my addictions pushed me into the darkness.

***

A boy wandered into the desert without his own desire. He wanted to help. He wanted to shepherd a truth into an unclouded grassland where the perpetrators of falseness would abandon their falseness in shame.

His story continues. A few thousand decades of seeds gave us these gardens. He gave us these gardens.

And yet still I wonder where he has gone. I wonder if he left the world to its own or if he stands outside the moonlight waiting.

***

Where would we be if we didn't ask questions?

Asleep in the sun or rotting the bottoms of rivers.

I didn't invent this line of inquiry. I only invented my world. A world of thieves in confession, a world of plentiful plates.

***

My hand was forced to meet my death, forced to embrace life, squeeze its juice. I learned to value the wretched and the doomed.

I might be grabbing a limb here and breaking it over my neck but even those in the thrall of madness are my kin. They came to me when I was naked, when I had nothing but scorn for my birth. They showed me how they slept at night in peace.

And like gods, they made the world in their image. Like patriarchs, they demanded obedience to their vision.

And so in an outbreak of commitment and passion, I prepared for my punishment. I felt ready for the trials of condemnation.

***

When I arose, I entered a kingdom of comprehension. No one is ever prepared. Nothing is honestly ready for today. Today knocks a feeble beggar on the threshold of tomorrow.

Even lies have their purpose. If presidents could not press an untruth from the grapes of their lips, who would kill the foreigners? Who would give their life?

I have lived a million miles of minefields and thrive in the throes of confusion. My determination has carried me to these desert gardens. I need a rest.

***

But a barefoot man sits on the subway steps. Dead or only looming, his hand betrays the existence of his hunger. Mexico City has no broken heart.

Besides, not only the living may show us a truth. Every palm – creased in death or by the sun – has a story.

And sometimes a dream must die.

In San Francisco, I assaulted my own nature when we stepped from the shadows on Van Ness street – and beat the shit out of strangers. May I confess in the heat of Jalisco far removed from those foolish causes that nothing was as it seemed, that none of my friendships gave comfort?

In those days outside the gardens, I granted each false foundation my reckless affection. The mob climbed down my throat and filled my guts. Had I the courage I would have confessed that my anger followed in the footsteps of hatred.

And how hatred could strangle my grace, maim my mercy, then slap me shocked against the killing wall.

***

But let's turn from the partition and find beauty on the boulevards. Take a look at:

Shoeshine men, trinket vendors, barely bearded drunkards, old ladies, tattooed convicts, heroin hookers, dancers, dog trainers,

painters, unionists, street corner preachers, cancer victims, homeless teachers, car washers, bottle breakers, cops and criminals, mayors, movie star gazers, tailors, carpenters, wine blotched boxers,

ex-marines, street stalkers, animal lovers, young mothers, children with gum for sale, snake handlers, fortune tellers, pineapple peddlers,

zealous critics in the tenement shadows of everything light.

All of them placed another viewpoint in my temperament. They enlarged my capacity for empathy.

And empathy illumes a dark vaulted heart, fills an empty bed with warmth, dampens a heated tongue.

Without it we hurl the needy into deeper wells, imprison the neglected in factories, trample justice with a herd of excuses, and throw families in the gutter to build a coliseum.

***

Imagine a five year old who thinks that truth is absolute. Imagine the ridicule. Imagine a five year old who swears to tell the truth and nothing but the truth for as long as his spirit shall remain.

He cannot see the implications as years grow into decades nor swear to keep to the banks of sensation and observation that flood him daily when gods in senility drool, when warm sands like ants of the desert gardens crawl over his feet, when nations throw spectacle and ritual slaughter from their bridges.

***

In my innocent age I volunteered to kill the enemy of the day. I dotted contracts with duty.

Don't tell me it was for nothing. I touched the mad face of flags.

And yet still I grieve for what I didn't do and for friends who burned up their lives and buried their futures. They bled while I wept my regret. They gave what I never could.

***

Many pleasures, the sun warms the roofs. Early morning, men shout in the street below my house, sell their foods and water.

I could gaze upon my sanctuary always, my spirit relaxed and uncoiled. But for chance of birth, I am the woman from Querétaro who begs her children in the street. How I welcome the harmony of her dignity when she smiles a shy elevation of lips, puts her hand out above the street bricks.

***

If I were a sculptor, I would carve a world of perpetual honesty, a world of fidelity with no exchange of blows.

But honesty loiters on hilltops. A family lives in peace. Their house and their children become their world.

They are simple and content – and the same as you and me. With the help of rain, Earth pushed them from seed (long dormant in the garden) and escorted them as they left their primitive desires to find a fresh future.

It may sound like I love everyone and I sometimes do. Yet I still rally my rage at our heartless humanity and summon a mighty impatience for fools.

***

A headline reveals another young man dead. My head packed with relentless obsession and nails, I question the ever changing rationale of war.

Look, I don't want to create a debate that Fords are better than Chevys, but the kid died for deceit that:

difference is evil

that God is small, has only one name

that enemies may soon burst into the inner chambers of our values when they already share our balconies and beds.

***

Now boys on my street climb the steps to the plaza and shout that old is the same as dead.

But if I may be permitted to say listen, listen:

I have been beneath the cities. I have crawled tunnels and over broken bricks. I have blackened my leather feet. I have been escorted by the flesh of god to a hall of dead Romans, known the accusation that their dust dead eyes delivered to me – and though passed, known fear of their retribution and awe of their power to persuade from the mausoleum that their crimes were kind, compassionate and wise.

One arm gripped by goodness, the other by hate. I have lain helpless on the slab.

But I escaped from a lifetime of catacombs.

***

It's time to surrender. I say with the strength of scaffolds that my life was worth it. I carried my joys and burdens with vigor.

A reward belongs to those who cast the day into its grave and breathe new life into the night.

Suffering has no god to blame, no deity to shame.

If anything, we create our own cross. From hilltops, when policy makers dictate who will live in ruins and who will slide their shoes over marble floors, we craft responses with our silence. We spread stains into the fabric of our cities.

***

Ordinary people buried under life's cargos stare at the sky. In the streets where the transports are heavy, they carry their children on their chests in the dark dusk of evening.

Without them, we are nothing, a windswept pile of October leaves. Without them, we have no home.

***

Sometimes a man comes to the end of his life before he dies. He sees ahead a world where bakers continue to make bread, horses continue to trample the grass, bells and steeples continue to call the hour, children continue to tilt their face to the rain.

It's not hard. When you have received the music of heavens and carried in your cups the incredible seeds of creation, it's easy to die, to leave your garden to its blooming.

What's not easy is to feel that underneath the lust, behind the trust in gods who may not give a whit for my legacy that I have been foolish and ill to break bread with 10,000 years that flash before my eyes like bolts of light when I stand upon

my terrace and donate my gifts to the indifference of masses who cast from false
faded love of popularity suffer.

***

It's time to take a census. It's time to consider. I am large, with many wonders and
contradictions.

I am evil. I am darkness beneath your umbrella. I am light.

I am mad and sane, have crossed a thousand islands in the sky.

I am mist that rises from mountain valleys to caress your eyes.

I am curves in the road that winds above the river.

I am the bird that pecks you on the head at night.

I am the butterfly that flies from your mouth when you speak.

I am a wing that flutters on the crow when the farmer takes aim.

I am a drop of spring water on your skin.

I am an angry rude spirit and have no hope.

I am Judas as he runs his rope over the branch.

I am an antelope in the field and the grass beneath his hoof.

I wear clothes that Solomon left behind when he ascended.

I hold a bloody birth sheet in my hands.

I preach into the sky and anoint the mud.

I buy a candy from a stranger when I have no hunger.

I am a caravan of wise men on their way to a birth.

I am a long line of ships.

I am a thousand pieces of glass beneath your naked feet, a thousand insistent demands, a thousand chunks of gravel in your throat and all the sweet notes that float from horns and strings in evening as the orchestra of birds and beasts begins to warble.

***

And it's time to admit this is my closing song. This is more than graffiti talking. I have shared skin with devils, have stretched my grasp to heaven. I have children on the outskirts of Texas and grandsons who play games with their lives.

My fear is that another fraudulent prophet of glory as salvation for your threadbare youth will step to the mic and spew claws from its mouth.

My fear is my grandsons will heed the call, and blindly sound another battle cry.

What can I say to them and all people that I have not already said?

I love you.

I want a better world for you.

May you realize a true and lasting peace.

***

In the beginning, I came to these gardens to lay my darkness down.

In the end, I have dragged you by the hair. I have chewed a hole in my disguise. It's time to put on my horse legs and ride. Many towns have not yet met me. A score of gods have yet to sympathize or make me red.

In my final fortune of footsteps, a gift of millenniums opens its mouth and bellows my name, and the name of every human being who put their beliefs to the test,

who pried creeds from their shells and like oysters slid them down their throats, who threw back the door when the beggars knocked, who planted a flower in the garden, who opened the borders of their arms,

who crossed a desert of mad whims to find a drop of rain, who gave themselves to life as if life were not a plaything nor a trifle but a large and splendid door that opens on a universe of passages that run as panthers though worlds full of sculptures and portraits of our bloodline standing as it does on the shore of our souls.

Listen. Our heritage calls across the water for our compassion and wisdom to grow freely from trees that every child from every continent and country may pick the garden fruit there.

And from this great nourishment, flourish.

ABOUT THE AUTHOR

Victor David Sandiego lives in the high desert of central Mexico where he walks the cities and mountains, plays odd time drums, writes, and studies. He is the founder of Subprimal Poetry Art, and the founder / editor of Dog Throat Journal. His work appears in various journals and on public radio.

For more information, see:

victordavid.com

dynamiccreed.com